INNOVATIVE PUBLISHING

THUGGZ
VALENTINE

BY

WAHIDA CLARK

Wahida Clark Presents Publishing
60 Evergreen Place
Suite 904A
East Orange, New Jersey 07018
1(866)910-6920
www.WClarkPublishing.com

Library of Congress Cataloging-In-Publication Data:
Thuggz Valentine by Wahida Clark
ISBN 13-digit 978-19366496-3-1 (Paper)
ISBN 10-digit 1936649632
ISBN 13-digit 978-1-944992-01-9
(Hardback)ISBN 10-digit 1944992014
ISBN 13-digit 978-1-936649-18-1 (eBook)
LCCN: 2015910467

1. New Jersey-2. Thug Life 3. Murder- 4. African American-Fiction- 5. Urban Fiction- 6. Natural Born Killers-
7. Gangster Disciples- 8. Prescription Drugs- 9. HIV- 10. AIDS-

Sr. Editors Linda Wilson, Latoya Smith and Keisha Caldwell
Proofreader Rosalind Hamilton
Printed in USA

THE END
Bless and Ebony

CHAPTER ONE

February 14
6:15 p.m.

Thuggz Valentine, mutherfuckaz!"

The ground shook from the explosion.

Kabooooooom!

The blast rattled the ground like an earthquake, igniting cars and SUVs, shattering store windows, knocking out the power, and setting off car alarms within a two-block downtown Newark radius. Several bystanders were killed, including a few police officers who'd had the two suspects surrounded, as well as every person inside the overturned bus, which was the source of the blast. People thought it was a terrorist attack.

It wasn't.

It was a standing ovation for Bless and Ebony. They embraced death on their own terms. They lived their last day on the edge and to the fullest. Even though it was filled with murder and mayhem.

Three minutes earlier . . .6:12 p.m.

"Fuck y'all!" Bless managed to yell out, despite the burning sensation of the bullet wounds and a natural sense of impending doom. His head rested on Ebony's lap while her back leaned against the underbelly of the overturned bus.

Ebony stroked his head. "Shhh baby. Save your energy."

Muffled cries and yells of anguish echoed from the passengers trapped inside. There was no escape. The bus had landed on the door side, destining everyone inside to a fiery fate. Desperate, the imprisoned riders beat furiously on sealed windows, too dazed and hurt by the crash to even come close to shattering them. Their hysterical eyes gazed at all the police surrounding them in a half moon formation. Officers shielded themselves behind open doors with automatic weapons, pistols, and shotguns all trained on Bless and Ebony. High above, a police helicopter hovered.

"It's over." Bless closed his eyes.

"No, baby, not yet. Remember what you said? Real gangstas never give up," she reminded him.

He forced a smile onto his lips. "You . . . you, could've saved yourself."

With tears running down her cheeks, she stroked his face. "Today has been the best day of my life. Before you, I didn't know what it really meant to be free. I am feeling totally alive. Anything after this would be a disappointment. I love you, Bless," she expressed, but she knew he hadn't heard her. She felt his body convulse, tighten, and then relax. She knew he was gone. She had been speaking to his soul. A soul she knew much deeper than even she was conscious of. Ebony held back every tear but one, which escaped down her cheek. She closed Bless's lifeless eyes with two fingers that resembled the peace sign, and then laid her gun on her leg. A tall, black detective stepped out of the police mob with his arms raised. He advanced slowly.

"Listen to me, Miss. Please. This can all end peacefully. I want to walk you out of this alive," he pleaded.

"Believe me . . . I plan to," Ebony said.

"That's good. Very good," he replied, missing the significance of her tone.

Ebony reached into Bless's pocket and pulled out his crumpled pack of Newport's and matches. "Don't shoot! Don't shoot! It's just a cigarette!" she bellowed at the itchy trigger-fingered officers.

Just a cigarette . . . She didn't smoke.

She put it in her mouth, lit it up, then inhaled a satisfying stream of smoke. When she exhaled, all the fear that she was harboring vanished.

"Now, I'm going to ask you to toss the gun over, okay?" She inhaled. "Not yet."

He shook his head. "No! I said now! Look around you." She did.

"It's over! There is nowhere to go!" he warned her.

Ebony glanced at all the stone-faced police squinting through scopes, with her head in the crosshairs. She took in all the gawking downtown onlookers, all while hearing the stifled cries of the people on the bus. And lastly, she looked up at the beautiful blue sky.

"Yeah, you right. There's nowhere to go . . ." she

remarked, andthen struck another match. "But up."

She and the cop exchanged glances. Yet, he strained at thematch. The realization hit him when he saw the leaking gas from the overturned bus pooling in the street and settling like a beached whale. His brown eyes widened in horror, taking in the implications of the lit match.

"Nooooo!" he yelled.But it was too late . . .

"Thuggz Valentine, mutherfuckaz!" she screamed, laughing asif life was one big joke.

Then . . . she tossed the match.

CHAPTER TWO

5:56 p.m.

The back of the ambulance swung wide and slammed into a parked car as Ebony fishtailed out of the hospital parking lot. Car alarms whooped loudly, but could hardly be heard over gunfire and screeching tires.

Boc! Boc! Boc! Boc!Boosh!

One of the back windows shattered as police opened up with multiple shots trying to stop the stolen ambulance and the wanted couple inside. "Gimme that gun!" Bless gritted, fighting through the pain. Ebony handed him the gun as she swung a hard left, picking up two more cruisers on the chase.

Bless staggered toward the back of the ambulance, thrown off balance by Ebony's wide maneuvers. The painkillers had him doped up, so he couldn't feel the bullets that would be forever lodged inside him. He braced himself against the wall and took aim through the same back window the police blew out. He let the gun go.

Boc! Boc! Boc!

8

He shot straight at the driver's face. The first bullet spiderwebbed the windshield, but the second shattered the officer's skull. Bless watched the driver's head snap back, a mist of blood painting the inside of the cracked windshield. The passenger tried to grab the wheel, but the cruiser slammed into a parked car, hurling the passenger through the windshield and breaking his neck against the car's hood.

"Mutherfuckin' right!" Bless shouted, proud of his handiwork. He knew he wouldn't live through this, so he was intent on taking as many souls with him to hell as he could.

"What happened?" Ebony called out.

"I just blew that muth . . . aaarrrggggh!" he groaned.

Bless had only turned his head for a second, but that was enough time for another police cruiser to zoom up close to the bumper of the ambulance and allow the passenger of the cruiser to snipe him through the window. The bullet pierced Bless on the left side of his chest and knocked him back onto the gurney.

"Oh my God, Bless! Talk to me!" Ebony yelled, wanting to jump up and run to him.

"Fuck! I got hit!"

Their situation was growing darker by the minute.

"Baby, just hold on. I got us!" Ebony vowed, slamming the accelerator to the floor.

More police cruisers poured into the chase from every side street she passed. In the distance, she could hear the beating wind. That could only mean one thing.

Helicopters.

She took a deep breath to fight back the tears, but her

mind continued to race. She remembered hearing somewhere that helicopters couldn't fly over airports, but she knew they were too far away from Newark Liberty International Airport. They had to lose the police on foot, or blend into a crowd. They had to disappear somehow, somewhere. *It's useless*, her mind told her.

Fuck you! Her spirit screamed back.

Ebony made a right so sharp, she damn near flipped the ambulance. Two police cruisers overshot the turn and sideswiped each other. Two more gone. But the police were like roaches. For every one taken out, there were ten more in hot pursuit.

"T-take 'em t-t-to the hood, bae," Bless gritted. "We . . . canlose 'em there."

Ebony looked at the speedometer leaning hard over 100. The downtown city stores, office buildings, people, hustle and bustle zipped by with the speed of a bullet. Up ahead she saw the road block. The police had the street clogged. Guns cocked, sights set. But Ebony wasn't about to stop. She gripped the steering wheel with both hands and focused dead ahead.

"She's going to ram us!""She's crazy!"

"Open fire!" the commanding officer barked. The overly anxious, adrenaline pumping cops began spraying the approaching ambulance.

At the last moment, Ebony swerved onto the sidewalk, crushing two pedestrians, but having no time to care. The move gave her enough space to skirt the blockade, ducking low as people dived aside as she sped past.

"Hahahaaaa!" she cackled like a mad woman, feeling the rush and energy of being totally alive. *Make it to the hood, make it to the hood, make it to the hood*, she kept telling herself like a mantra to whichever god was listening.

Behind her, squad cars flashing blue and white lights were still on her tail. Some so close, they bumped her bumper trying to make her lose control. They were everywhere. Every second she felt more and more like she was drowning, descending into the depths of hopelessness, sinking into further doom.

And then she realized . . .

From the moment they met, she knew they were destined for tragedy. But today hadn't been about winning, it had been about living. It had been about a love deeper than she had ever knownand was now ready to die for. It was about embracing the moment, no matter the outcome. Once that thought went through her mind, her whole body seemed to relax and unravel, like an unclenched fist. A smile spread across her face like the sun shining through a cloudy day.

"Bless," she called out. "You still with me?" "Yeah, sweetness."

"I love you."

She heard him laugh that laugh that made her pussy wet, andthis moment was no exception.

"That's obvious," he replied. "I love you too." "Sing our song, bae," she requested one last time.

"Shorty, I'm there for you anytime you need me, for real girl, it's me and your world, believe me," he rapped, the energy of the moment enough to make him forget the pain.

As he rapped, her mind played back to the highlights of

the day.

And to think, I started this morning wanting to die.
Ebony smiled.

She never saw the bus.

It came from her blind side. She slammed her foot onto
the brake and so did the bus driver. He panicked and threw
the wheel hard to the left. The automatic air brakes
locked up, causing the bus to tip over, landing on its side.
It began sliding toward her with almost as much velocity as
it had when it was on its wheels. The people inside were
tossed around like popcorn kernels as sparks shot up the
whole length of the bus's side. It slammed into the
ambulance, pushing it full steam ahead into the side of
a corner store, pinning the transport vehicle so hard, it
almost crushed it like an accordion.

The force of the collision virtually knocked Ebony out.
The only thing that kept her conscious was the love in her
heart and her sheer will to get them to safety. Bless lay
dazed, coughing up blood. Ebony pulled herself free of the
front seat and staggered to the back. She grabbed Bless's
arm.

"No, ma, go! You still have a chance. Leave me
here," he agonized, blood running down his chin.

"Say that again, and I'll shoot you myself," Ebony spat,
taking the gun out of his hand. She put his arm around her
neck and embraced him around the waist. "Bae—"

"Stop—"

"But we still got a chance, baby," she tried to convince
him, hoping against hope that she could speak it into
existence.

"Damn, I love you, girl." He coughed, giving it all he

had as they climbed out the back of the ambulance.

The little leap from the bumper to the ground proved too much for his weak knees and his whole body collapsed. The only thing keeping him up was Ebony. They made it around the bus.

"I told you I got us, boo." She giggled, enjoying the moment, despite the obvious.

Whatever window of escape they had, quickly closed as police swarmed the area. They kept a buffer zone, but their formation saidone thing . . .

This was the end.

They both paused and looked out at the sea of blue before them. Neither was scared, but only one of them knew what they were going to do.

Ebony spotted the gas leak.

To her, it was as easy as accepting destiny. Bless coughed so hard, his whole body shook. She held him tighter.

"Come on, Bless. Sit down. Let's have a picnic," she joked, while hoping they wouldn't become the barbecue.

They settled down only a few feet from the gas leak. The police formation was 100 feet away from them. Bless laid his head on herlap. She laid her head against the bus's underbelly.

"It's . . . it's over," Bless managed to get out.

But, that was something they had both known for a long time.

CHAPTER THREE

5:26 p.m.

E bony sat in the Bentley shivering, and it wasn't just from her wearing a pair of tan boy shorts and a yellow tank top in the middle of winter. Her attachment to Bless had become like a drug, and she felt withdrawal symptoms. Now that he was gone, she could only focus on getting that next fix.

Gone.

The word seemed so final, so absolute, and it made her want to die on the spot. Even though he wasn't gone, her meaning of gone meant that he wasn't with her now, where she needed him to be. She felt helpless and alone, like life was slowly draining from her like a balloon. Still, Ebony imagined his tongue between her legs, his dick deep inside her, his hands all over her, caressing her everywhere. He had known. Even when she'd said no, he knew she meant yes. No one but one other man had ever touched her like that. Made her feel so wanted, so desired, so loved. It felt good to have that void filled.

She found her own fingers pushing aside the thin

material of her tan, silk boy shorts. Her juices pooled, slicking her hand, and before she knew it, she reclined the front seat, cocked her foot up on the dashboard, and forced two fingers inside her throbbingpussy.

"Ohhh, Bless!" she moaned, imagining her fingers were his. "Open up to me, sweetness. Give it all to me." She heard his voice in her head.

Ebony spread her legs wider and arched her back, sliding a thirdfinger inside herself. She twisted her digits in and out, back and forth, the whole time seeing Bless in her mind's eye, dicking her down.

Suck on my thumb while you take this dick, she imagined him saying.

Placing her left thumb in her mouth, she grinded her hips into her three-finger stroke.

"Yes, Bless, deeper. Oh fuck yeah! Right-right there," she gasped, totally lost in her own fantasy.

"Fuck! This pussy is so wet. Make it cum for me!"

"Y-yes, daddy, yesssssssss," Ebony replied, popping her pussy faster and faster, harder and harder, bucking her hips until herpussy exploded with such force it squirted all over the steering wheel and dashboard.

Sexually quenched, her whole body slumped, but when she opened her eyes and cold reality slapped her stunned face, her stomach knotted and she hugged the steering wheel and began to sob.

"Bless," she cried.

It was over. Her mind repeated, "Die . . . Die . . . Die . . ."

No.

Something inside her spoke up again. *No.* It was loud,

clear, and denied her access to the weak little girl hidden inside.

Bitch, go get your man! Her resolve compelled her, unwilling to take no for an answer.

If we're gonna die, we're gonna die in his arms, the crazed voice vowed, slowly spreading through her veins, filling her with fearlessness, vigor, and I-Don't-Give-A-Fuck energy, as it made its way all through her being.

The tears stopped falling. Ebony sat up, focused. Thinking, *But how?*

Ebony started the car with no more of a plan than the directions to the hospital. As she drove, she wondered how in the world she was going to get Bless out of police custody without a weapon. Hell, she didn't even have on a pair of shoes! The thought made her burst out laughing hysterically, and the laughter helped her overcome the last of the tension left in her body.

She looked at her own eyes in the rearview mirror, remembering Bless's words. *"Your eyes slant just like a cats. I bet there's a panther in there somewhere,"* he had said while she rode his dick.

"We're about to find out," the words rolled off her tongue. The light turned green. Her mind said, "Go!"

Ebony drove to the hospital and turned into the parking lot, her head on swivel and her eyes peeled. A few police cruisers were parked around the main entrance, and when she drove around they were near the emergency entrance as well.

"Shit!" she spat as she pulled into a parking space backward. She knew her face was recognizable because of surveillance videos from the robberies. Besides, they had seen her when they had snatched up Bless. There was no way she could walk through the front door.

Then she saw him. A janitor. Her sharp gaze zoned in on a young, black dude with frizzy cornrows that badly needed to be redone. The new growth had sprouted up like weeds between garden rows. He stood in the open door of a maintenance entrance smoking a cigarette.

"Perfect," she purred.

Ebony got out of the car. The concrete chilled her bare feet. The wind whipping through the parking lot instantly hardened her nipples, making it obvious that no bra covered her perky C-cup breasts. They stood out like elevator buttons through her tank top. Ebony knew she didn't have much of an ass, but her boy shorts had her dark-chocolate thighs looking delicious and lickable. With her fresh French pedicure on her tiny feet, she knew the total package would get his attention.

"Damn, lil' mama, you okay?" he asked, exhaling a stream of smoke, looking her up and down. "Where are your shoes?"

"Long story. Can I have one of those?" she asked in a flirtatious manner.

"You can have the pack with those thick thighs," he replied, inhaling. "But what you gonna give me in return?"

She snickered and bit her bottom lip seductively. "What do I gotta give?"

"Shit, I think you got plenty.""I might."

He looked her over again. Her short, natural afro and double- dipped chocolate skin tone wasn't his cup of tea, but being a man, he wasn't about to turn down easy pussy.

"Well uh, why don't we step inside, so we can figure out how we gonna help each other." He proposed, getting his mack on.

"I thought you'd never ask." She giggled girlishly. "Lead the way."

As soon as she stepped inside the dimly lit hallway, a gang of butterflies burst open in her gut like a bad appendix. She immediately began to size him up. He was at least six foot one and 220 pounds. Ebony, on the other hand, stood five foot five and barely weighed 135 pounds. She knew she would have to overpower him, and possibly kill him. And it wouldn't be as easy as it was before, with Bless by her side. *I wish he was here*, her heart sighed wistfully.

He is, the hum in her heart's spirit answered.

They came to a long flight of steps that descended into the bowels of the hospital.

"Where are you taking me?" she asked, feigning innocence.

"To my cozy little man-cave. I might have some shoes for you down here," he lied with a chuckle, lusting for her as he peered over his shoulder.

Ebony didn't hesitate. She gripped both hand rails tight, and with all her might, lifted herself, swinging her feet. With as much force as she could muster, she kicked the janitor in the small of his back.

"Oomph!" he grunted. His body pitched forward with such velocity that when his face hit the rail, it put a nasty gash on his forehead and knocked out two of his teeth. He bounced off the rail, falling backward, arms flailing, grasping and gripping for anything. As he teetered, his fear-filled eyes mixed with surprise once they met Ebony's for a fraction of a second. Hers said nothing. She wasn't angry. It was simply business. She watched as he tumbled down the long flight of stairs. His body twisted in all the wrong ways.

He toppled, head over heels, fracturing his neck with a nasty snap as his head banged one of the concrete steps. His momentum flung him end over end like a rag doll, until he lay motionless at the bottom of the stairs. Ebony quickly ran down behind him, then squatted beside him to see if he was dead. He wasn't.

"Y-y-you dirty b-b-b-bitch, I. Can't. Feel. My. Legs. My neck," he stammered, blood trickling from his mouth.

"You'll be all right." She looked around the storage room surrounded by supplies, and she spotted a shovel. Casually, she crossed the room, grabbed it, hoisted it over her shoulder then wentback to him.

"Who sent you here?" he mumbled.

"Shut up!" she spat, then lifted the shovel high above her head. "Wait! I can't fuckin' move. You still want to kill me? Who
sent you here?"

"I told you to shut the fuck up!" She brought the shovel down inthe middle of his face.

The sharp side of the shovel split his skull so deep; Ebony wondered if she could pull the shovel out of his head. Blood shot everywhere as she allowed the shovel to slip from her hands. The sight of the blood invigorated her. She felt like she had superhuman strength. But the shit smell assaulted her nostrils. She knew he'd released his bowels during the process of the death blow.

Job complete, she searched the room until she found what she was looking for. "Yes!" she squealed, happy to find some nurse scrubs, booties for her feet, and a stethoscope to complete the disguise. Speedily, she outfitted herself in the oversized scrubs, then headed for the opposite door which opened into a hallway. She looked both ways before heading left. The antiseptic smell made her follow her nose to the medical examination room, or what most people mistakenly called the morgue. There wasn't a breathing soul in sight, but a dead body of an old man lay on a gurney. Beside the body was a set of scalpels, razor sharp, gleaming so brightly they seemed to wink at her. But it was onlythe shine of the overhead light kissing off the stainless steel.

Now she was armed.

Ebony headed for the elevator.

"I'm coming, baby," she whispered like a prayer as she watchedthe numbers on the panel change.

Ding!

The door swooshed open on the third floor. Nurses bustled backand forth while hospital visitors sought solace and good news. She looked around for tell-tale signs of police presence posted outside aroom. When she didn't see one, she stopped a middle aged white nurse as she sauntered by. Her name tag read RN, Blitz.

"Excuse me. Nurse Blitz, I know you're busy, I have a quick question. They—"

"Where is your name tag young lady?" Nurse Blitz questioned. Ebony fought to keep her cool. She looked down at the uniform.

"It must be in my purse. Silly me. I will go and get it."

The nurse sighed, as if to say, *Always an excuse.* "What do you need?"

"I know you are busy, and I really am sorry." Ebony leaned in as if she was getting ready to tell her a secret. "They may have brought my best friend in here. If the police bring in an arrestee, what floor would they take him to?"

"Downstairs. Second floor," the nurse was now becoming suspicious. "What did you say your name was?"

"We met before. Karen from the weekend shift. Nurse Blitz, letme let you get back to your rounds."

Ebony left her standing there and headed for the elevators. She looked back and saw that Ms. Blitz went about her business. With caution still a priority, Ebony took the stairs instead of the elevator. When she emerged on the second floor, she saw the police detail down the hall, sitting outside the door.

"This is it!" she mumbled. Taking a deep breath, she held her head up high and walked down the hall.

The white officer saw her approaching and stood up. "Excuse me. Are you the nurse assigned to this room?" he questioned.

Despite her nervousness, she had come too close to turn back, so she went for all she knew. "Do you think I'd be going in here if I wasn't?" she spat back, neck snake-rolling, ghetto style. "As bad as my feet hurt, and not to mention I don't want to be here. I ain't got time for this, okay? And I'm working a double."

The whole time she spoke she gripped both scalpels, thinking, *Please don't let him recognize me, please don't let him recognize me, please don't . . .*

He held up his hands in mock surrender and chuckled. "Hey, no problem. Believe me—I don't want to be here either. Just doing my job."

"Then excuse you while I do mine," she huffed, bypassing him and going inside.

As soon as she walked in, her heart skipped a beat seeing Bless lying in the bed handcuffed to the rail. Eyes closed. But as soon as she stepped beside the bed, he opened his eyes. He kept his poker face, but his beaming eyes said it all. *This chick is the goddamn truth. She sho' nuff is ride or die!*

"Excuse me, nurse."

Ebony turned to see another white cop sitting in a chair in the corner. "Yes?"

"Is there any way I could get you to bring me some water?" he asked, holding up an empty Styrofoam cup. "I've been dying of thirst."

Ebony hit him with that sweet killer smile. "Sure, if I get your help with this."

The officer got up and approached. "No problem," he replied, stopping beside her. "Help with what?"

"With this!" She pulled the bloodied scalpel from her pocket, clutching it like a claw and swiped it straight across his eyes.

"Aaaarrrgggh!" he screamed, his eyeballs lacerated and leaking like punctured egg yolk, running blood and plasma. Ebony knew she only had seconds between the yell and the second cop rushing the room. She went straight for the gun. The cop grabbed her hand.

"You bitch!"

She sliced him across the fingers; his pinky severed and

spurting. Snatching his gun from his holster just as the second officer burst through the door, she barely had time to kick the safety off before he tried to go for his gun.

Boc! Boc! Boc!

All three shots hit him in the chest, knocking him to the ground.

She started to turn back to Bless.

"Baby, he a cop! He gotta have on a vest!" Bless yelled. Sure enough, when she turned her head, the officer rose up, trying to take aim.

Boc! Boc!

This time she put both in his head, sending blood skittering across the floor and brain matter clinging to the wall.

"Damn, ma, I can't believe this shit! Goddamn, I love you, girl." Bless cackled like a maniac in the electric chair after the governor called.

"You better!" Her heart was racing. Swiftly, she retrieved the keys to the handcuffs, uncuffed him from the bed, then helped him up.

"Can you walk?" she asked."Naw, but I can run!"

His humor forced her to smile as she helped him to the door. She bent down and gave him the second gun then arm in arm, they were out the door.

"Freeze!"

Was the first thing they heard.

One more officer.

Dozens of eyeballs gazing at them. You could almost hear a pin drop except for the lady on the phone talking about, "They shootin'up in the hospital!"

Boc! Boc! Boc!

23

Bless banged on him. One more body.

Thump!

The officer's body hit the floor, and the bullets meant for him pierced through the chest of the nurse closest to him. Visitors scattered and surrendered. The screams echoed off the gray concrete walls inside the exit staircase. "You a fast learner," Bless remarked as they descended the stairs.

"The panther just came out." She winked.

He smiled even though he was in pain. "I knew it would."

The way he was draped over her shoulder, he could see straight down her blouse and tank top. Her succulent breasts bounced freely. "Damn, I wish we had time for a quickie."

Ebony chuckled. "Hold that thought until we get to Bermuda." "Aruba."

"Both!"

Their spirits were high, only because they were dreaming and detached from reality.

They stepped out onto the first floor. A group of officers were running toward the stairwell. Word obviously had reached the unit. Both concealed their weapons when they saw they weren't needed. But the breather didn't last long.

"There they go!" The first officer to spot them shouted out!

They looked back just in time to see a gang of blue stampede through the door. Neither hesitated.

Boc! Boc! Boc! Boc! Boc! Boc!

Both opened fire. A bullet found a target in an elderly lady's face. Her old wrinkled flesh exploded.

Pandemonium broke out. People were running, dodging, and ducking wildly, so the police couldn't get a shot off. But the murderous couple could.

Boc! Boc! Click!

Ebony's gun locked. It was empty. She and Bless left the emergency floor headed to the ambulance bay. She snatched the gun from Bless and turned it on the worker as he emerged from the back of the ambulance. She was feeling herself. The gun fire, the violence felt welcoming.

Boc!

The shot blew through his jaw, dropping him like a Mike Tyson punch. His body tumbled off the edge of the bay.

"Where the fuck did you learn to shoot like that? Girl, gimme my gun back?" Bless kidded. They both jumped inside the ambulance.

"I got this, bae. You just relax and watch mama!" she replied. The key was in the ignition. Just as Bless slammed the doors,

several police swarmed the ambulance bay, guns blazing.

Bless got low. Shots ricocheted off the vehicle's body. "Drive, baby!" he hollered.

She punched it. The back of the ambulance swung wide and slammed into a parked car as Ebony fishtailed it out of the parking lot.

"Aruba here we come!" Bless bellowed. "You mean Bermuda!"

Their young laughter echoed inside the ambulance. Their destiny doomed.

CHAPTER FOUR

4:14 p.m.

Bless and Ebony were all over each other as soon as they fell through the door of the hotel suite. The door banged against the wall as Bless pinned Ebony to it, tonguing her down and squeezing her ass through her skin tight jeans.

"Ba—" *Smack, smack,* their lips met. "Bae . . . the . . . door . . . is . . . open," Ebony reminded him, kicking out of her Jimmy Choos on the spot.

"So!" he replied, pulling back from her juicy lips just long enough to pull his shirt off over his head. "Oh, so you shy and modest all of a sudden? You saying I should have bent you over in that glass elevator and beat the pussy up from the back?"

"You better watch yo' mouth," she taunted. "I dare you to do it."

He quickly grabbed her hand and started to leave the room. Ebony laughed and pulled him back inside, closing the door behind them. She jumped into his arms and wrapped her legs around his waist.

"I can't believe what we did! Oh my God!" Ebony gasped, high off loving her life at the moment.

Bless dropped her onto the pillow top bed. She bounced and giggled just like a kid having fun.

"I told you, ma. This is our day! A Thuggz Valentine! We ain't takin' no for an answer!" he boasted proudly.

She took one look at those money green eyes, suckable lips, andcocoa complexion and her pussy started to cream.

"Damn, boy. I'ma fuck the shit outta you," Ebony purred lustfully.

"Not if I fuck the shit outta you first," he shot back.

She slowly pulled her jeans off. Teasingly, she eased her panties down over her hips, stepping out one leg and then the other before kicking them across the floor. "Do you like what you see?" She stood in front of him posing seductively.

"I do. But I need you to lay down for me."

And she did, spread eagle. "How do you like this?"

He turned the leather Gucci satchel he was holding upside down, dumping all the jewelry, loose multi-colored diamonds, and money all over her body. The diamonds sparkled in the sunlight and looked like candy rain as they fell on Ebony's naked body as she giggled. She rolled and frolicked in the goods as Bless stripped down to his chiseled frame, his hard nine inches pointing straight at her like a Mandingo spear.

"Damn I love your scent," Bless said as he ran his nose along her dripping pussy lips.

"Bless, wait. I think I got a diamond in my ass," she snickered.

Bless cocked her legs over his shoulders and stuck his

tongue in her ass. A pink diamond fell out, but Bless paid no attention because he was too concentrated on *her* pink diamond.

"Ewwwww fuck, Bless! Your tongue in my assss," she cooed, the sensation had her wanting to melt into the bed.

He ran his tongue all around her puckered back door. Then slurped and sucked it until Ebony thought she would lose her mind.

"Ba-ba-ba-bbabbbbyyyy. Nooooo," she groaned because Bless slipped his thumb in her ass and at the same time began sucking her clit. She grabbed the bed and tried to squirm away, head thrashing from side to side. She couldn't take it anymore and came incredibly hard in his face. She felt like the room was spinning.

"Wait . . . Wait . . . Wait," she begged, but Bless wasn't hearing it. He was already turning her over.

He gripped his dick at the base, spread her eagle on her stomach, then gutted her with one hard, powerful thrust. Ebony bit the bed to keep from crying out loud enough for the angels up in the heavens above to know he had hit her spot dead on. Bless got in a push-up position, so he could watch his fat dick punish her tight-ass pussy.

"Arch your back, ma. Take this dick," he grunted. "O-o-okay I—oohhhhh fuck!" Ebony squealed.

Bless pulled her up on her knees, pulling her coily hair with both hands, and rode that pussy from the back like a pony. "Gimme that pussy!"

"It's yours, baby. I swear to God, it's yours!" she gushed. "I love you, girl!"

"I love you, toooo00," she replied, just as she burst all over his dick, then looked over her shoulder. After catching her breath she said, "Now I want to get on top."

Bless smirked, then pulled out of her. Her pussy was so wet, his withdrawal sounded like the suck of a suction cup. Bless lay on his back as Ebony threw her leg over him. She grabbed his creamy dick, then guided it inside of her. She licked the juices off the palm of her hand as she began to find her rhythm. Sitting straight up, she braced herself with her hands on his rippled stomach and looked him in the eyes.

"You saved me . . . you know . . . ohhh fuck . . . do . . . you know that?" she moaned.

"You saved me, too," he replied solemnly.

"Promise me, no matter wh-what happens, you'll never—" "Never," he answered before she could even finish, because he

knew exactly what she was going to say.

"Ebony threw her head back, cocked one leg up and rode his dick with total abandon. She couldn't get enough of every painful but pleasure-filled stroke.

"Cum in your pussy. Cum all in me. I want to have your baby," Ebony gasped. "Even if it's only make believe."

The words made her tear up, because deep down, something told her it would never be. Bless wiped away her tears even as he long-stroked her pussy. Then when he felt the quiver in his stomach, he grinded into her as deep as he could go, then filled her womb with his seed.

Ebony lay on his chest. He started to move.

"No don't. I just want to feel you inside of me," she remarked. He smiled and kissed her on the forehead. "You okay?"

She nodded. "Scared?"

Lifting her head, she smiled into his eyes then replied, "Not anymore." She paused. "Why did you take me?"

Bless shrugged. "You could identify me."

Ebony laughed and playfully bit his chin. "You were wearing amask."

He returned her smile and caressed her cheek with his thumbs."Gut instinct. Aren't you scared?"

"Half of me is scared I'm gonna wake up, but the other half is scared that I'm not asleep," she admitted. Her love and fear createdthe perfect mix for anxiety.

Bless lifted her chin with his finger, kissed her nose then her lips, and said, "Don't worry, baby. By this time tomorrow, we'll bebutt naked on somebody's beach."

"Then we really are going to jail, with your nasty self," she teased.

He laughed and slapped her round, shapely ass. "I'm nasty?"

Ebony smiled and winked. She got up reluctantly and grabbed her pants. "I'm going to get some ice. You want a soda or something?"

"Just get me whateva you drinkin'," he answered, rolling over on his stomach.

Not feeling like squeezing into her tight-ass jeans, she grabbed her shorts from off the dresser and her tank top that was tangled upwith her blouse.

"You want anything else?" she asked over her shoulder as she headed for the door, grabbing the ice bucket from off the shelf.

"Yeah, walk nasty for me." He chuckled.

Ebony giggled then tooted her ass with an exaggerated

switch.

Once in the hallway, she headed for the ice maker, her bare feet padding over the soft carpet. She hummed the melody of Jill Scott's "The Way," thinking how crazy life was, and how good it felt to be loved.

"Shit!" she spat. "All this money for a room and they ain't got no ice!" She dropped the lid shut. The exit door was right beside the ice maker. Ebony shrugged and pushed open the door to the stairwell. The concrete was cold to her feet, but she was determined to get some ice. She descended to the floor below. The ice machine was in the same place. She cracked the lid and peered inside.

"'Bout time." She chuckled and filled her bucket.

Right by the ice-maker was a window, giving a full view of the outside parking lot. Multiple cop cars and a SWAT van were in clear view.

Her breath caught in her lungs. There was no doubt who they were there for.

How did they find us so soon? The thought started its way to the forefront of her mind, but she quickly pushed it to the back because she knew time was of the essence.

The bucket tumbled from her hand as she pushed open the exit door. The first thing she heard was the military precision of multiple footsteps echoing off the concrete stairs. She peeped over the rail. Two floors below, a long line of blue helmets snaked down two more floors. She sprinted up the stairs, taking them by threes. Panting, she started to snatch open the door, but instead she obeyed the little voice inside of her screaming, "You better look first!"

She did.

A six-man team of trained officers exited the elevators.

Ebony's heart pounded with angst. She ached to scream out for Bless because she knew he was oblivious to the blue storm about to gather outside their room door.

The sound of approaching boots got closer. She turned and ran up one more flight of stairs, the whole time trying to figure out what to do.

As soon as she opened the doors, she saw it. Right before the ice maker. The fire alarm. Without hesitation, she grabbed the handle and yanked it down. It screamed soprano-style, filling the hotel with the shrill sound of the steady high-pitched vibration. In her mind it was more than a ring—a mechanical version of her voice screaming, "Blessssssssssss!"

And he heard.

Bless had been lying on his stomach, dozing off. As soon as the alarm shrieked, his eyes popped open. The way he was lying, the first thing he saw was the front door. A small movement at the base of the door caught his eye. At first, he thought it was some kind of bug, but that thought was quickly replaced by the realization that it was another type of pest. The kind of telescopic, snake-necked surveillance camera police used to see under doors before they entered. Bless and the bug saw each other at the same time.

"Oh shit!" Bless snapped.

"Go! Go! Go!" the SWAT team leader boomed.

At the same time that Bless was reaching for the gun lying beside him with one hand and the edge of the mattress with the other, the police were taking the door clean off the hinges with one blow from the fifty pound swing bar.

Boom!

Boc! Boc! Boc!

Bless held the edge of the mattress as he rolled onto the floor, using it as a shield, while he let off shots over the top. All three shots hit two of the officers, but they were so heavily armored, the bullets did little more than spark off their shields. But their shots found flesh.

Boc! Boc! Boc! Boc! Boc!

Shots came from several weapons simultaneously, blowing through the mattress and Bless, too.

"Aaarrrggghhh!" he grumbled as a bullet tore through his upper arm, chest, and hip. One head shot whizzed by so close, he could feel the heat of the momentum as it went by and blew out the hotel window.

Boosh!

The last thing he saw before he blacked out were six automaticsall aimed at his face as he lay on the floor, dazed and dying.

When Ebony heard the shots, she jumped like each was going through her. Since numerous nosy but frightened hotel guests werepouring into the hallways, it was easy to get lost in the crowd.

"This way, ladies and gentlemen. Please don't panic," one officer said as he stood on the landing of the room's floor directingthe hotel guests.

Ebony had to fight the urge to push past him and run down the hall to be a ride or die chick for her man, but she knew she'd nevermake it. She kept her head low and made her way down the stairs. When she came out into the lobby and was heading toward the front door, she noticed a familiar face talking to someone whom she was sure was a cop.

That's how they knew! Her mind screamed, eyeing the red- headed white bitch from the lobby who checked them in. She had ratted them out! Ebony rushed outside, and the brisk wind hit her full in the face, but she was too numb to feel it.

Bless . . .

Her whole spirit shrank. She felt she was to blame. If she hadn'tgone out to get ice, she would've been there, and together they could've done something. Now, all she could do was pray that Bless wasn't dead.

Ten minutes later, she was able to release her breath. She watched as the police brought Bless out on a stretcher, the EMS working while holding up an I.V. She wasn't near enough to see his face, but she was close enough to at least know that he was alive. That was enough for now.

She turned away and made it to the Bentley. Ebony glanced around before heading towards it. How could they miss a stolen Bentley? They couldn't be that stupid. Or was it a trap? The thought never even occurred to her that maybe a higher power was watching over her. She looked around some more. No one seemed to be watching the car. *Fuck it. I ain't got nothing to lose at this point. And I don't have no other way to get around. I gotta save Bless. I gotta save him.* She jogged to the Bentley and climbed inside. Reaching under the mat, she pulled out the key and started the car, staring out into nowhere.

Where would she go? Where could she go? Nothing about her former life was worth returning to. Anything after Bless would be a disappointment. In such a short period of time, he had become her world, her life. Now she sat alone feeling like she couldn't breathe. First Terrence. Now Bless.

"Think girl! Think!" she urged herself, but her mind was numb.

Ebony pulled out driving aimlessly. The tears streamed, rushing fast and uncontrollably, until she was forced to pull over.

"Bless, I'm so sorry," she sobbed. "What can I do? I don't know what to do!" She rolled up in the seat, crying and shivering, hoping God would save the new love of her life.

CHAPTER FIVE

2:30 p.m.

W e gotta get out of this car," Bless remarked as they zoomed along the highway.

"I was just thinking the same thing," Ebony said, eating her fries.

Bless looked at her with a proud grin. "You even startin' tothink like a gangsta."

Ebony laughed, basking in his pride like a little girl lost in her daddy's love.

"Okay then, gangsta, what do you suggest?" he asked.

Still munching, Ebony thought for a minute. She took a sip of her soda and asked, "Do you know how to steal one?"

He scrunched up his face with arrogant disdain. "I'm fromNewark, ain't I? It's in my DNA. But if we steal, then we have to worry about OnStar and all that other GPS shit. One call and they can kill the engine from space," he explained.

She shrugged because she was acquiring a taste for violence. "Then just jack somebody and stuff them in the trunk until we get finished with the ride."

"Same problem."

"Then I don't know," she said, frustrated.

"What do you mean you don't know? Think. What would you do if it was just you?" Bless pressed.

Hating the pressure and resenting the challenge, Ebony went over it from every angle. Take a bus? Train? No, too hot. Plane?

Hell no. She was just about to give up, when it popped in her head like a rabbit out of a hole.

"If we get it off a car lot, OnStar won't be activated," she announced proudly, like she had just solved $E=mc^2$.

Bless chuckled. "Duh! Smart ass! Why you think we gettin' off of this exit?"

She looked up, and in the near distance spotted several car dealerships ahead. "Shut up, nigga! I got your duh!" She laughed, playfully mushing him in the head.

They bypassed the Buick and Subaru dealership, heading for the Nissan dealership on the right. That is until something on their left caught their attention.

An exotic car dealership.

What caught their eye wasn't the row of gleaming Continental's facing the highway. It was the sky blue and cream Continental GT sitting in the middle of the showroom floor on a rotating platform like the spinning plate in a microwave. Just its presentation made it look like forbidden fruit slowly revolving. The gleam off the grill practically blinded them and their mutual smile said it all.

Bless made a left into the parking lot.

"Boy, a damn Bentley? That's gonna cause too much attention." Her heart beat with excitement.

"Fuck it! Grab the bags, bae," Bless told her while he reloaded the .40 caliber clip.

Ebony grabbed the leather Gucci satchel, then they both got out. Hand in hand, they entered the showroom. A short Italian guy with a receding hairline, wearing an expensive suit approached them. At first he took them as mere window shoppers, but when he saw the diamond Breitling watch on Bless's arm and the size of the large diamond in his ear, he figured him to be another ghetto superstar and assumed the satchel was full of money.

He was only half right.

"Hey, how are ya? Jeffrey Tucci, but you can call me Jeff," he said, shaking Bless's hand. "Welcome, and thank you for coming in. What can I do for you?"

Bless answered by nodding at the Continental.

Jeffrey heard cash registers ringing in his head. "She is a beaut, isn't she? Come on over, let me introduce you." He chuckled. "Mr."

"Bless. Call me Bless."

"Oh okay. Entertainer I take it?" Jeffery asked.

"No doubt. How'd you guess?" Bless was being sarcastic but Jeffrey paid him no attention. He was only concerned about making a sale.

The three of them stepped onto the rotating platform. Jeffrey hit a switch and it stopped. Ebony peered inside the open window, taking in the luxury, including the new car smell.

"Let me get that for you, pretty lady," Jeffrey offered, opening the door for Ebony.

She slid in the sumptuous leather seat, and it felt like a soothing bubble bath. "Ooooh, baby! You were right. This is the one," Ebony raved, wrapping her fingers around the steering wheel.

"You like that, huh?" Jeffrey smiled, knowing if a woman liked it, the car was as good as sold.

"I love it!" Ebony squealed.

"Folks, this is the two-seater Continental GT3.R. We're talking the 571 hp version of the twin turbo 4.0 liter V.8 engine. This one here is state of art. The epitome of class, speed, and luxury." He spent the next few minutes showing them the buttons, bells, and whistles.

Bless then leaned against the body, glancing around, taking in the rest of the showroom. He noticed two other salesmen. One was a petite white woman talking to an Asian couple. The other was a tall, slim white man with slick hair and sporting several gold chains and rings. He was sitting at his desk on the phone.

"Hey, I'm sold! If my lady likes it, I love it," Bless remarked.

Jeffrey rubbed his hands together. "Music to my ears. Shall we get down to the nitty-gritty? I promise I'll be gentle. How much are you ready to put down on it?"

Bless shrugged. "Money's no object. "We'll take it."

Jeffrey's body tensed up, and he tried his best not to frown. He had dealt with some extravagantly rich people, but no matter how much money they had, they would still haggle to get a better price. His gut flashed red, but his greed tossed the warning out into the universe. *He has to be one of those rapper guys.*

"Between you and me, I wanna do right by you. Shoot your best shot," he said, not knowing the irony of his own words.

Bless smiled at Ebony, and she bit her bottom lip to suppress a laugh.

"No . . . I don't think you understand. Money is *no* object," Bless repeated, then pulled out the .40 caliber and aimed it at Jeffrey's face. "I said we'll take it."

"What the hell!" Jeffrey yelped, throwing up his hands.

His loud cry drew the attention of the other two salesmen and the Asian couple. Ebony pulled out her nine and hopped out of the car, crossing the room to cover the others.

"Everybody! Kiss the fuckin' floor now!" she ordered, waving the gun from head to head. She felt like a natural born killer.

No one hesitated. They took a dive quicker than a washed up boxer for the mob, and ate the carpet. Ebony went from person to person confiscating cell phones.

"Where's the keys?" Bless asked the salesman.

Jeffrey pointed, too scared to speak. Ebony followed his finger to a big board draped with keys. She spotted the keys marked "Showroom Floor," then came back to the car holding the keys outto Bless.

"You can drive." He winked at her as he took their salesman's phone out of his pocket. "Thanks, Jeff. Nice doin' business with you."

With that, Bless went around to the passenger seat and Ebony started the car with a roar. He closed the door, and then turned on the car radio.

"Boy, all we had to do was take it for a test drive!" she squealedwith excitement.

"Fuck that. Too easy. We on a mission. A mission to live this day to its fullest. Now punch it." Bless couldn't help but snicker at what they had just pulled off.

Ebony floored the pedal as hard as she could, causing the wheels to screech and smoke before it shot across the showroom floor then straight through the decorated glass window.

Booshhhh!

Ebony laughed like life was tickling her insides. She loved the feeling of seeing the power machine smash its way free. The wheels fishtailed slightly as it hit the pavement, then went from zero to sixty in a blink. Suddenly, the verses of Hov and Beyoncé began booming from the speakers.

All I need in this life of sin—

Bless sang along. "Is me and my girlfriend. "Down to ride tothe very end, it's me and my girlfriend!" Ebony sang along as well,inserting 'boyfriend' in the appropriate spot.

They laughed their asses off as they zoomed down the highway.

Several miles later, Bless turned down the radio. "Pull off at the next exit. We gettin' a room."

Ebony looked at him quizzically. "Why? We need to put as much distance between—"

Bless shook his head. "That's exactly how the police think we're thinkin'. Runnin' for our lives, hidin' out in sleazy hotels. Fuck that! We ain't goin' out like that. We gonna get us a five-star hotel suite and hide out in plain sight. Then we'll leave town on thetrain," Bless explained. Ebony understood his logic. It made sense, but her woman's intuition said it was more to it than that, and it was. Bless didn't want to die running. He wanted to die loving.

They passed up several hotels until they came to a brand new Hilton just like Bless said. Hide in plain sight. Ebony bypassed valet and found a parking spot, pulled the key from the ignition, and started to pocket the key.

"No," Bless told her."No?" she echoed.

He shook his head. "Leave the key. Put it under the seat. We take one with us. You never know what the situation will be when we leave. Always leave a key in the getaway car," he schooled her.

"What if somebody finds it?"

He laughed. "Nobody will expect a muthafucka to leave the key in a hunnid somethin' thousand dollar car!"

Ebony shook her head with a snicker. "You think you got all the sense, don't ya? The car is hot and it's a Bentley Bless!"

"Trust me girl. In plain sight."

They got out and headed inside. They went straight to the counter. While Bless got the room, Ebony felt like someone was watching her. Casually she looked around until she spotted a red- headed white woman. She knew she had been staring, because as soon as Ebony looked, the woman glanced away. Ebony pretended not to look a second time, but out of her peripheral she saw this woman look again.

As soon as Bless had the key card, she said, "Don't look now. Wait. Okay look now! Tell me if you see the red-headed bitch by the couches over there!"

Bless played it off, then gazed around the lobby. "What redhead?"

Ebony looked and the redhead was gone. "Bae, I don't like this. I'm telling you that red-headed bitch over there is all in our grill."

"Don't sweat it, ma. White people always stare at niggas." He chuckled. "We at the Hilton."

Ebony let it go, but deep down it would nag her until . . .

Ding!

The elevator came and they disappeared inside. As the doors closed, Ebony scanned the lobby once more. Not seeing the woman, Ebony started to doubt it herself.

But she shouldn't have.

The red-headed woman had dipped outside and tipped 911. She had the crime stopper app on her phone. The city was within that radius. The alert had showed her the jewelry store surveillance video, along with a composite sketch of what the couple looked like. She recognized them instantly.

"Nine-one-one," the operator droned.

"Yes, I think I just saw the two people from the story on the news. It's them!"

CHAPTER SIX

12:13 p.m.

Bless rolled over from his ten minute nap to find Ebony standing at the hotel window wrapped in a white fluffy towel, looking out at the passing traffic.

"I thought you'd be gone by now," Bless remarked, only half- joking.

"And go where?" she replied without turning around, reminding him of an earlier conversation. Bless could tell by her tone that there was something wrong. Naked, he got up, came up behind her and wrapped his arms around her waist and kissed her neck.

"You okay?" he asked.

There was a soft pause. "I'm not afraid anymore.""I can tell."

"Of anything."

Bless understood completely. He slipped his hands inside the towel and caressed her breasts. Ebony closed her eyes, leaned her head back against his chest and basked in his touch.

44

"With you, I feel like I can do anything," she stated. He kissed her behind the ear. "Yes you can."

Pulling the drapes closed, he let her towel hit the floor, turned her to him and eyed her from head to toe. "Damn you beautiful, ma."

She smiled. "I know that . . . now. But I need to face what mademe feel so ugly."

"You mean . . ."

Ebony nodded. "Don't forget, before we leave I gotta make thatstop."

"Then let me take a shower and we out."

While Bless showered, Ebony's mind kept returning to the many days in the closet . . . The darkness. The tears. The fear. It became clear to her that, in a way, she had been trapped in that closet her whole life, and she vowed to herself never to be trapped again.

******

I wrote these words for everyone who struggles in their youth . .

The words to Lauryn Hill's "Everything is Everything" kept Ebony's head bobbing like she was in church as they rode across town. Bless kept his eyes peeled for any signs of the police, knowing they were in an area where they could easily be trapped off. "Turn right here," Ebony instructed him.

They turned into a rundown neighborhood on a back street in Montclair lined with houses that had seen better days. Garbage lined the sidewalks. It was obvious it hadn't been picked up in weeks. Half-rusted cars sat on cinderblocks, which dirty-faced kidsused for recreation.

"It's the yellow house in the middle of the block. Park right there," she told him.

Peep the mixture Where hip hop meets scripture
Develop a negative into a positive picture

Lauryn's words were the last Ebony heard before Bless cut offthe car. She sat for a minute and gazed at the house. The yellow aluminum siding had faced the sun for years, making the house looked piss-colored. The grass only grew in weeded clumps. The rest of the yard was nothing but dirt and cigarette butts. Wild cats ran around like they owned the place, some sitting on their haunches watching Ebony watch them.

"This place hasn't changed one bit," Ebony remarked, tone voidof emotion.

"You want me to go with you?" Bless questioned.

"No. I have to do this by myself," she replied. Then after a shortpause that resembled a deep breath, she opened the door and stepped out.

The cats didn't run when she approached. The dirty gray one had the audacity to hunch up and hiss. Ebony ignored it and climbed the rickety, wooden porch and then knocked on the door. Several moments later, a little boy who looked no more than seven answered.

"You my mama?" the little boy asked with such intense hope, she knew that, that was what he prayed for every night.

She wanted to scoop him up in her arms and give him a big hug,but she wasn't there to show mercy.

"Where's Miss Cat?"

"In the back. You look like my mama. You my mama?"

"I'm not your mama," Ebony replied, more coldly than she felt.

When she stepped inside, the past enveloped her like a mist. It was like stepping back in time. The house still smelled like stale cigarettes and stale pork rinds. The sound of *The Price is Right* reverberated from Miss Cat's bedroom. The house was still a mess because of all the piles of clothes, some clean, some dirty, strewn all over the place. The only difference was the faces of the victims. The foster kids sat around, being sucked dry. All three were in the living room, a little boy and two girls, one who looked no more than nine, the other at least twelve. They all watched her wordlessly. Ebony walked past them and then down the hall to the last bedroom on the left. She pushed open the door and stood in the doorway. Miss Cat lay on the bed looking like a beached whale, much bigger than Ebony remembered. Her hair was totally gray. Other than that, she still looked like Della Reese.

"Bitch, what I tell you 'bout comin' in here without knockin'?" Miss Cat spat, not looking up from the TV.

"Fuck you!" Ebony hissed, her throat dry and tight.

She hated Miss Cat for being able to easily arouse the fear in her. Ebony foolishly thought that after all this time, and all that she had been through, she would have the toughness needed to stand up to her torturer. But she didn't.

When Miss Cat glanced at her, the recognition colored her features. She grinned a knowing grin. "Well, well, well, look here. If it ain't America's Most Wanted." Miss Cat chuckled, then hit her cigarette. A cat jumped up from behind the bed and snuggled next to Miss Cat. She stroked the feline lovingly. Ebony eyed the cat with contempt.

"Ain't you gonna say nothin'? I seen you on the news, you dumb bitch. You done killed a cop, huh? I always knew you wouldn't be shit, but I ain't know you'd get yourself killed on death row!" Miss Cat laughed at her own joke, taking a hit from the cigarette again.

"I came to say good-bye. For both of us," Ebony seethed, pulling her nine from her waist.

Miss Cat laughed. "Looka here. The bitch gotta gun! What you gonna do with that? Shoot me? You a killer now, huh? You think that shit scare me? You nappy-headed ass black bitch! You always been a little nappy-headed ass black bitch and you ain't never gonna be nothin' but a little nappy-headed ass black bitch!"

Inside, Ebony trembled. She aimed the gun at Miss Cat's face then stepped forward, picked up Miss Cat's phone and dialed 911.

"Come get these kids. The bitch is dead," Ebony said as soon assomeone answered.

"Hello? What? Who is this?" the operator questioned.

Ebony dropped the phone on the bed. Miss Cat's smile disappeared. The look in her eyes told her this wasn't the same little Ebony that she called herself raising.

"Hold up now! I didn't realize you were that upset," Miss Cat pled, stubbing out her cigarette. "I was just teasin'. You know . . . for old times' sake."

Ebony smirked. "Exactly. This is for old times' sake."

Boc! Boc! Boc! Boc!

Three shots split Miss Cat's skull, sending blood shooting out of her head like a volcano. Her eyes went cross as she slumped to the bed. The fourth shot turned the cat in her lap into a bloody fur ball. Ebony grabbed Miss Cat's purse off the bed and dumped it out. A wad of money fell out. The money she got from the state that the kids never saw a dime of. She picked up the money,turned, then stopped in her tracks because the three kids were standing in the door watching her, expressionless. They had seen itall. Ebony walked over and handed the money to the oldest. They stepped aside. Ebony walked through them.

"Will you be my mommy?" the little boy asked.

"Be your own mommy," Ebony replied without malice. She walked out the door.

The dirty gray cat had been licking its paw. It stopped mid-lickto hiss at Ebony again. This time she didn't ignore it.

Boc!

One shot took the animal's head clean off. The rest of the bodyslumped, twitching. She kept it moving.

She got in the car. Bless looked at her. "You good?"

"She knew about us. She said we was all over the news."

Bless nodded. "Not surprised. We definitely gotta leave townASAP."

He pulled off, and Ebony watched her past disappear forever, as the oldest girl stood in the door watching her drive off.

CHAPTER NINE

BACK TO EBONY ... THE CHILDHOOD

The Psychiatrist's Office

U h oh, you don't want that one. She's sick. Real sick." Miss Cat chuckled, standing in the doorway counting the money the man just handed her.

"Why not?" he wanted to know, the lust in his eyes so thick, it made them look bloodshot.

He was standing over nine-year-old Ebony while she lay in her bed, covers pulled up to her neck, terrified. In the bed beside her was an eight-year-old light-skinned girl and a nine-year-old Spanish girl.

"Willie, what the hell I say? She sick. Leave it at that."

Willie cursed under his breath. He had already molested the other two girls on various nights, but he was drunk, and the ugly little black girl had his eye.

"Fuck it, I'll take Allison. Come on here, girl," he huffed, taking the light-skinned girl and leading her out of the room.

Allison got up without a fuss. She already knew what Miss Cat would do to her if she did.

Ebony watched her leave, and her eyes welled up with tears for her. She knew that Allison hated what the men did to her. Especially Willie. He made Allison hurt between her legs and he liked to punch and slap the girls, especially when he was drunk. Like he was that night.

Miss Cat closed the door, and the room was once again cloaked in darkness. Maria, the Spanish girl sat up. Ebony could see her pretty butter-complexioned skin in the dark, and she envied Maria.

"I don't see why he wanted you, wit' your ugly black self. And you stink! You think I don't know what you got? You a AIDS baby! I hope you die," Maria spat, bullying Ebony as she usually did. Ebony knew she was just mad because Willie had picked Allison over her. Even at such a young age, Maria had resigned herself to the sick fate her beauty destined for her. She was used to men being inside her. Her father had begun molesting her when she was six. So in her mind, she was supposed to be chosen, even though the act itself made her feel dirty.

The walls of the house were thin, so Ebony could hear Willie's pig-like grunts, Allison's mouse-like whispers and the slamming of the headboard. Deep down though, Ebony wondered what it felt like—a thought that came from never being chosen by any of the pedophiles that came to visit. The other girls were always chosen because they were pretty. She wondered if a man's thing made you feel pretty inside. She knew it was wrong, but to her young mind, everything in her life was wrong.

Ebony had dozed off, and when she opened her eyes, Allison was back in the bed crying.

"I wish you'd shut up. People tryin' to sleep," Maria huffed, turning over to face the wall.

Ebony got up and did what she usually did. She got in bed with Allison and held her while she cried. It didn't matter that Allison would pick on her just like the other girls did. What mattered was, if no one would love her, Ebony always took the opportunity to love someone else in need.

"Shhh, don't cry. It's over now," Ebony comforted her.

"It–it hurts so bad. He . . . he did it in my butt," Allison cried.

Later, when her bleeding rectum wouldn't heal, Miss Cat was forced to take her to a hood doctor to get her stitches. The pain wasalmost unbearable.

Ebony cradled her like her mother used to do her when she was hurting. "I have a trick," Ebony said, wiping Allison's tears one night.

"What?"

"A trick for Mr. Willie. The next time he comes, I'm going togo in your place," Ebony whispered in her ear.

Allison looked at her. "You what?"

"Shhh, not so loud. I'm going in your place. I'm gonna make Willie sick, so he never comes back again," Ebony announced, proud of her plan.

Allison thought of all the foul things Willie did to her. Although she really didn't care about the ugly little black girl, she wouldn't wish Willie on her worst enemy.

"No, you can't. It won't work. Miss Cat will get us," Allison protested.

"Not if you do what I say," Ebony convinced her. She cupped her hands around Allison's ear and whispered her plan.

Willie came back to Miss Cat's house as soon as he had his paycheck. Since he had turned out his stepdaughter, he couldn't getenough of underage pussy.

"Bitch, open the door. Big Willie is ready for them youngfillies." He cackled as he lay on Miss Cat's doorbell.

She let him in and led him straight to the young girls' bedroom. She had a couple of thirteen-year-old girls, but to Willie, they were too old. He went straight to the young girls' bedroom.

Maria only had on her bra and panties, sitting Indian-style onthe bed. She was determined to get chosen. Allison was wearing a long pajama top, listening to her iPod.

"Where's Ebony?" Miss Cat questioned when she noticed that Ebony's bed was empty.

"In the bathroom," Allison replied, just like they planned.

Willie was just about to pick Maria, when Allison bit her bottom lip seductively and gave Willie a brazen look he couldn't resist.

"Yeah, you ready ain't you, lil' mama? Come on here then," he leered, handing Miss Cat the money.

Allison scrambled off the bed and took his hand. "Bitch!" Maria pouted as the door closed.

Willie led Allison into the bedroom at the end of the hall. Once they were inside and the door was closed, it was pitch black. Hefelt Allison let go of his hand, and in the darkness he lost even her shadow.

"Where you go, girl?" he called out.

"I'm right here," a high-pitched voice replied.

The voice sounded like Allison, but he wasn't sure. His lust decided it didn't matter. The voice was coming from the bed. He felt his way over and his hand brushed against skin. His hand moved up and down until he realized she was naked.

"Oh, here you are, huh?" He chuckled, taking his pants down and stroking his dick to full erection. "And here's Big Willie!" He pushed her little legs apart and positioned himself on top of her, but when he tried to penetrate, she was much too tight, nowhere close to what she had been.

"Damn, bitch! What you got, a new pussy?"

For Ebony, the pain was excruciating. As he shoved his massive meat inside her, she wanted to cry out, but she didn't want to alert him to the switch. Her whole body felt like it was ripping in half ashe forced all of his length up in her.

Willie didn't last two minutes.

"Goddamn, girl! Was that yo' ass? Them stitches got you tight!"

Just then, the door flew open and light from the hallway cut across the bed, exposing the scam. Miss Cat's eyes widened as she yelled out, "Ebony! Awwww shit, Willie!"

Willie looked down and saw Ebony underneath him and the bed was covered in blood. "What the fuck? Where the hell yo' blackass come from?" Willie exclaimed.

Miss Cat flipped on the light switch and found Allison squatting in the corner. "You lil' bitch!" she bellowed and lunged at Allison, but Allison slipped under her grasp and ran from the room.

She knew her girls too well. Miss Cat had sensed

something was up and had gone looking for Ebony in the bathroom. When she didn't find her there, she searched the whole house. Still not finding her, she knew there was only one place she could be.

Willie jumped up looking at all the blood on his midsection. Miss Cat had turned beet red. Willie took one look at the expression on her face and knew something was wrong.

"Cat . . . when you said this lil' bitch was sick, what youmean?" He was pulling up his pants.

"Oh my God, Willie! Oh my God!" Miss Cat stammered, shaking her head.

Ebony lay on the bed, sore, but deep down she felt good. He wanted her ugly, and she gave him the ugly.

"W-w-what did you mean?" Willie stammered, shaking with fear at what his mind knew was coming.

"She . . . she got the virus!"

"AIDS?" he shrieked, voice higher than Prince's.

Willie's knees buckled and he damn near fainted. He grabbed the edge of the dresser to keep him steady.

"Oh Lord Jesus! Lord Je-sus! AIDS!" he muttered, until his eyes fell on Ebony and the little girl was smirking! "Bitch, I'ma kill you!"

He lunged at Ebony, fists balled, ready to beat her senseless, until he felt the cold steel at his temple. It froze him like a kiss of ice.

"Un-uh, no nigga. Anybody doin' any killin' up in this muhfucka, it's gonna be me!" Miss Cat hissed.

Willie slowly backed away from Ebony, hands raised, tears cascading down his cheeks.

"Miss Cat, AIDS? This bitch gave me AIDS? That

bitch is evil!"

"She may be, but she my evil," Miss Cat spat. Not that she cared about Ebony, but the state paid too well for her to let him hurt her. "Now, you get out of here and don't never come back, ya hear?"

Willie grabbed his jacket and got the hell out of there. Then Miss Cat turned to Ebony, and the look in her eyes wiped any trace of a smirk off Ebony's face.

"So bitch, you think you got all the goddamn sense, huh? Well, I got something for your ass fo' sho'!"

The psych tried to maintain his professional detachment, but blurted, "You tried to infect someone? And on purpose?"

"God gave it to me on purpose, didn't he?" Ebony shot right back. "It may've been a mistake, but it wasn't my mistake, so why should I suffer? Why should he make people suffer and not suffer himself?"

"That doesn't make it right!"

"No, but it damn sure makes us even," Ebony countered. "And Dr. Jenson, I didn't come to be judged."

Dr. Jenson sighed and took off his glasses.

"I'm–I'm sorry. It's just . . . morally. How can you . . . justify .

. never mind," he concluded, finally placing his glasses back on and trying to regain his composure. He was not expecting this conversation. "So when she said she had something for you, what was it?"

"The closet." "Closet?"

Ebony nodded. "Miss Cat . . . she would lock me in the closet for days. Sometimes she wouldn't feed me. The closet was worse than hell for me. There was a hole where rats would run in and out of. They-they would bite me. To this day I'm terrified of rats."

"Did you feel you deserved it?" he asked. "You're judging again," she replied. "No, really. How did it make you feel?"

Ebony looked him dead in the eyes and said, "It made me want to kill again."

CHAPTER EIGHT

11:34 a.m.

"Whhat's Valentine's Day without diamonds?" Bless smirked with that mischievous twinkle in his eyes.

Those light brown eyes that she had quickly become unable to resist.

"You're crazy. You know that, right?" Ebony remarked, but feeling the plan oh so much.

"Naw, ma. Look around you," he told her. "Almost everybody in this world wants to be able to break out of their boring little existence and just say fuck it! Ya heard? Just take what you want. Not work for it, not earn it, not deserve it, don't even ask for it. Just fuckin' take that shit, feel me? And if this ain't that moment for us, then when? Our backs are against the wall. Where do we go from here? It's me and you against the world. So that's why I say fuck it!"

As Bless spoke, Ebony looked out at the people walking by. On their faces, the telltale marks of being exactly what Bless said they were . . . trapped. She knew that life all too well. She looked at the front of the jewelry store. The display in the window winked at her as if asking, *What are you waiting for?*

Ebony looked at Bless. "Let's do it!" She giggled. "So what do I do?"

"Follow my lead. And make believe you are playing a scene in the movies."

Ebony giggled again. "Alright. Let's do it!" Ebony put her game face on.

Click! Clack!

That was the sound of Bless cocking back the .40. "Fuck it!" he said, full of zeal.

They hopped out of the car and cut across the throngs of people

flowing along and entered the jewelry store. Inside, were three people: one middle-aged blonde behind the counter showing a ring to a Latino man, and a tall black woman with a super short orange cut perusing the bracelet display.

Bless and Ebony wasted no time pulling out their guns and controlling the scene.

"Y'all seen it before, and if you haven't, follow orders and it'll all be over real soon! Eat the fuckin' carpet!" Bless bellowed as he hopped the counter.

He grabbed the blonde saleswoman by the hair and slammed her face into the display case, breaking her nose. Blood sprayed across the glass. He let her fall, dazed, onto the floor.

Ebony put the gun to the Latino man's head. "Are you deaf?

Down! Now!"

"O–o–okay," he stammered, dropping to his belly.

59

The black lady didn't have to be told twice. "Please, don't shoot! I'm cooperating!" she cried.

Bless quickly ran to the back of the store checking for anyone else. He came to a closed door and kicked it open. Inside was a short, stubby Jewish dude with a bad toupée and a jeweler's loupe up to his right eye.

"Hey!" he yelped in surprise, before Bless broke his jaw with the handle of the pistol. He slumped to the floor spitting blood and teeth.

"Open the safe!" Bless ordered. "Please don't—"

Boc!

Bless aimed the gun at his knee and blew blood and bone allover the man's rumpled but expensive suit.

"Okaaaaayyyyyy!" he bellowed, grabbing his knee and writhingin agony.

"Now!"

The man dragged himself over to the heavy floor safe in thecorner. With trembling hands, he spun the dial, messing up twice.

Bless put the gun to the back of his head. "Crack the fuckin'safe, or I'll crack your fuckin' skull!"

Click!

The old man pulled the handle. Inside, was a stack of miniature gold bars, several stacks of money, and a black velvet bag. Bless snatched the bag out and untied the drawstring. Inside, were multi- colored diamonds. Bless's dick got hard.

"Gotdamn it! I hit the jackpot!" He chuckled.

"J–j–just go. You've got what you want. Now go," the old man stuttered, grimacing in pain.

"Sorry, pop. I'ma go, but not before you." "Huh?"

Boc! Boc!

Two shots, point blank to the man's eye sockets blew his brains out the top of his head. His body tumbled back and slumped in the corner.

Bless grabbed the shopping bag and swept the money and the gold into the bag. Then he placed the diamonds on top. When he came out and made it up front, Ebony was running around with a black leather Gucci satchel that she had taken from the black lady and was emptying the contents of every display tray into it.

"Ohh, baby, look!" she exclaimed, holding up a watch. "Look what I got you!"

He slid the diamond-encrusted Brietling onto his wrist and admired the shimmer in the light.

"Wait until you see what I got for you," he replied, holding up the bag, then placing it inside the satchel.

They laughed, enjoying the moment as if what they were doing was perfectly fine and they didn't have a care in the world.

"What did you do to my grandfather?" the blonde sobbed. "Please tell me he's okay!"

She had heard the gunshots, and deep down she knew something bad had happened. Her heart just didn't want to accept it. Bless raised the gun.

"Noooo!" the woman cried, shielding her face with her hand.

Boc! Boc!

The bullets blew into her chest, killing her in a matter of seconds. Her body twitched then lay still.

"What is the matter with you children? How can you kill someone in cold bold like that?" The black lady cried out.

"Simple. Just like this." Bless told her.

Boc! Boc!

He spun and put one in the back of the black woman's head, painting the thick, plush, cream carpet, crimson.

"The Lord is my shepherd, I shall not want," the Latino man prayed feverishly.

The whole time, Ebony stood there transfixed. Watching the whole scene, mesmerized. She felt it so deep in her bones, she shivered.

Bless looked at her and read the expression on her face. "Bae.""Huh?"

Remember when you asked me what it felt like to kill somebody?"

"Uh-huh . . . yes."

He lowered his weapon. "You tell me." Ebony looked at him, wide-eyed. "What?"

Bless tucked away his pistol, then walked over and positioned himself behind Ebony. He leaned in close to her ear and said, "Your turn." He wrapped his arms around her, lifted her hands to grip the gun with both hands, and helped her aim the gun at the kneeling Latino.

"What are you doing?" she asked, butterflies fluttering in her belly.

"It's what you doin'," Bless answered. "Please no, don't do this!" the man begged.

"Hear that? You hear how he's beggin' for his life? How gangsta is that? He prayin' to God, but he should be prayin' to you," Bless remarked with a chuckle.

Ebony couldn't lie. The fear in the man's eyes made her feel a surge of power she had never felt before. She licked her lips and took a deep breath to try to calm her racing heart.

"Tell me you ain't feelin' yourself right now," Bless said, kissing her on the neck. "Tell me it ain't makin' your pussy wet."

It was. The feeling of being in control was a powerful aphrodisiac.

Ebony imagined herself back at the motel, staring at herself in the mirror, her own nakedness being reflected back at her. Bless, behind her, his arms wrapped around her, just like in the jewelry store. Her pussy was soaked just reminiscing about it.

Bless slipped two fingers inside her. "Damn, your pussy creamy."

She cocked her foot up on the sink, watching him finger fuck herto the knuckle.

"Tell me I'm a bad bitch," she moaned.

"You a bad bitch, bae. You say whether he live or die. Wrap your finger around the trigger," Bless instructed.

She snaked her finger around the clit of metal.

She squeezed her own clit as Bless twisted his fingers in and out, in and out, her pussy juices dripping down her thigh.

"Squeeze it," he told her, "Watch how good it feels."

"Squeeze it. Watch how good it feels," Bless's voice was filled with lust in her ear.

Tears lined the Latino's cheeks. "Have mercy on my soul!" he begged.

"Make it cum for daddy!"

"Make it cum for daddy."

She squeezed and felt her breath being taken away. She

felt the sensation all through her body.

She squeezed and felt the jolt of the recall travel the length of her arm, then explode all over her body. The bullet launched matrix-style, entering straight through the Latino's open, protestingmouth and exited with a sickening splat out the back of his neck.

She squeezed again. Bless fingered her harder and faster."Again," he urged.

"Again!" he demanded.

Soon the rhythm of the squeeze and the smell of blood filling the air, sent Ebony over the edge, and she squeezed until the clip was empty and the man's dead body was no more than a bloody lump of flesh.

"Goddamn, you a bad bitch!"

******

Jewelry Heist A Success . . . Checked into the Marriott.

Her pussy came fast and furious. The only thing holding her up was Bless's strong arms. She was as limp as a rag doll when he bent her over the sink, so close to the mirror she was almost kissing her own reflection. Bless ran his tongue down the crack of her ass, sucked the sensitive spot between her pussy and her asshole until her whole body shook. Then he slid his tongue onto her clit.

"Ssssss, oh Bless, fuckkkkkkk!" She creamed, her pussy cumming instantly as her clit and pussy lips got thoroughly explored while he three-fingered her vigorously. Ebony cried out; it felt heavenly.

"What are you doing to me?" she gasped, lost in her feelings. "Whatever you want," he answered sincerely.

"I want your dick in me, baby," Ebony whispered

feverishly.

Bless stood and turned her around, sitting her on the sink and cocking one leg up on his shoulder, the other one on his chest. He leaned and began to suck on her toes as he guided his throbbing bell head into her pussy. Ebony watched it, inch by inch, disappearing up to the balls. Her toes curled.

"I love how you feel inside me. Tell me it's good to you," she urged.

He stuck his fingers in her mouth so she could taste her own juices.

"This pussy is the best, baby," Bless grunted.

The feeling of his nuts slapping against her asshole sent her over the edge and made her cum again.

"Daddy w-wait," she begged, breathlessly, dizzy.

She wrapped her legs around his waist and her arms around his neck, tonguing him down like she had lost something down his throat.

Bless picked her up and carried her across the room, and then laid her down onto the bed. He started at her forehead then proceeded to cover her body with licks and kisses. By the time he reached her belly button, she gasped, "I love you, Bless. I love youso much."

He stopped and looked at her sincerely. "I love you, too."

"Make love to me again, baby."

He slid back inside her, then long-dicked her until they both came together. Ebony laid her head on his chest and threw her leg over his, rubbing it up and down. After a short silence, with them basking in the aroma of their own juices, Ebony blurted out, "Fuck heaven!"

Bless laughed hard because he felt the same way. "No doubt, mama. I'm feelin' you."

"For real though. If heaven is supposed to be this amazing place where you don't want for nothin', then I don't need it, because I'm there right now," Ebony explained, meaning every word, and every word touched Bless's heart.

He kissed the top of her head. "I wish we woulda met under different circumstances."

She lifted up and looked at him. "Why? I know. It's no way in hell we gonna walk away from this is it?" *Then it's no use in me telling you that I'm infected.*

The look on her face was hopeful and trusting. It was almost child-like in its innocence, but Bless couldn't bring himself todisappoint her.

"There's a possibility," he lied. "It's just . . . I don't know. I wish I coulda put my swag down."

"Oh, believe me"—she giggled, as she laid her head back on hischest, "You definitely did that."

He smiled. "Naw, not like that. I mean like . . . took you out. I always wanted to take a bit—I mean—my lady to Coney Island. Don't ask me why, I just did. My step parents took me one time when I was around eight, and I saw this dude win his chick a stuffed animal. Ever since then, I was like, I'ma do that for mygirl. I just never had one worthy of a stuffed . . . you asleep?" he asked, because he could hear her breathing.

"Huh?"

"You was asleep."

"No I wasn't," she slurred, on her way back to la-la land.He chuckled. "Then I did my job."

She wasn't even alert to reply. He lay there for a moment, until the weight of her head on his arm started to make it go to sleep. He got up and crossed the room to get his clothes. All of a sudden he got the chills.

Where do we go from here? Bless thought.

He had started the day with a simple robbery, and now he was the city's most wanted cop killer.

"I can't believe he was a fuckin' cop," he mumbled as he pulled the blunt of exotic from his pocket.

He was far from giving up, but he knew they had a long way to go before they'd be anywhere close to getting out of the jam that they were in. Every cop in the city was on their trail.

Bless shook his head at the assessment of the situation as he checked his pants pockets for his lighter. At that moment, Ebony sighed in her sleep, then turned over facing him. *She looks so beautiful asleep. Will she look that beautiful dead?* He contemplated killing her.

He hurriedly shook off the thought. "We gonna do our damndest to get out of this," he promised himself.

Again, he looked at her, wondering why he had gotten her mixed up in all this bullshit.

Because I can't leave without her, his heart answered.

It wasn't just her beauty, because to most she wasn't beautiful. With her jet-black skin, short, kinky afro, and petite yet slightly pudgy build, no one would ever mistake her for a beauty queen. But what made her beautiful to him was how it all came together. From her low slung hips, to her ballerina stride, the slight gap between her two front teeth that went so well with the cat-like slant of her eyes. To him, she was the most beautiful woman in the world and that was all that counted.

When he couldn't find his lighter in his pocket, he started to double check, remembering he had given it to Ebony. He picked up her purse and reached in for the lighter, but his eyes caught on to a sealed peach-colored envelope addressed to the city morgue.

"The morgue?" he read with a scowl.

He pulled out the letter and opened it. When he read it the first time, he couldn't believe his eyes. When he read it a second time, his whole stomach turned inside out, realizing that she was on some bullshit. Immediately, he stalked across the room and shook Ebony violently.

"Ay yo!" He loomed over her, face twisted up.

She woke with a startle, jumping up, ready to break out.

"What? What's wrong? Bless, why are you looking at me like that?" she questioned, his demeanor giving her a sinking feeling.

He flung the letter in her face. "Fuck kind of shit you on, huh? What's this all about? You givin' up on me? The least you could've done is told me!" Bless roared with a rage that seemed to shake the walls. "Real gangstas *never* give up!"

Ebony's heart sank as she picked up the letter. "Baby, I swear it's not like that! I—"

"Not like that? What the fuck is it like?" "I wrote this before we met!"

At that moment, the only sound was the hum of the refrigerator.

He gazed at her momentarily, then asked, "Before?"

Ebony nodded. Bless shook his head, trying to make sense of the last few minutes.

"But . . . why would you want to kill yourself?" he asked, his voice softening with concern.

Ebony took a deep breath to fight back the tears, but it didn't work. She tried to wipe them away. "I-I don't know what to say . .

. I-you wouldn't understand." She sniffled. "I'm already dead. Andso are you."

Bless sat beside her on the bed. He wiped her tears with his thumb, then tilted her head up. "Ebony, talk to me. Make meunderstand," he urged. Not having a clue that she was talkingabout the virus instead of their situation.

Ebony shook her head, looking off and out of the slightly parteddrapes. She pulled her knees up to her chest and wrapped her arms around them, rocking herself gently.

"Bless . . . there's so much you don't know about me. The things I've been through, how hard life has been for me . . . I'm twenty-five years old, and for as long as I can remember, every morning started with me cursing the fact that I woke up . . . trying to think of reasons not to kill myself," Ebony explained between sobs.

"Wow, ma . . . that's deep. But I just can't see you killin' yourself. Look at you yo, you beautiful."

Ebony shook her head and lowered her eyes. "I-I'm not."Bless lifted her head. "Yes, you are."

Ebony tried to muster a smile. "To you . . . yes. But for real, today is the second time in my life that I felt needed or desired. I had a man, but he died in a plane crash. He was the first person who ever loved me, other than my mama, Bless. Do you know how bad that hurts? And then to be reminded of it over and over." Ebony wiped her eyes with the back of her hand. "I-I was raised by a foster woman, or at least, that's what the state called her. To me, she was just a person that got paid to hurt me. She never did shit for me, never spent a dime on me. She had this house full of cats, and she would feed them better than me. She hated me, and it made me hate myself."

Bless pulled her into his arms and allowed her to cry it all out. He didn't say a word, didn't even know what to say, so he let the love speak through his silent but strong embrace.

"She . . . she hurt me soooo bad. She made me hate my skin. I would get in the tub sometimes and scrub until I bled, hoping I could scrub the blackness off. Every day, if I did any little thing wrong, she would beat me senseless. Bless, you just don't know what hell is," Ebony cried.

"We all got our own hell, ma," Bless replied, thinking of the pain that he had felt. "But why did you address it to the morgue?"

"Because I didn't have anybody who cared enough to send itto."

As she cried, he lay back with her, keeping her close, then he began to rap to soothe her.

Nothing makes a man feel better than a woman, Queen with a crown that be down for whatever . . .

. . . Even when the skies are gray,

I'ma rub you on your back and say baby it'll be okay . .

They both drifted into a light sleep.

A little while later, Ebony got up and took a shower, her mind replaying the events of the day. She started the day wanting to die; now she wanted this moment to exist forever. It was all because of Bless. She had never met

70

anyone like him. A man that fulfilled, thrilled her, and chilled her all at the same time. Terrence was one thing, but there was something deeper about Bless that she felt, but couldn't explain. After she dried off, she stood watching him sleep. "Please God, help us make it out of this. I want to spend my life makin' this man as happy as he's made me," she prayed. "Don't take him away from me."

But despite the love in her heart, she couldn't get past the hate etched in her soul. As she stood looking out the motel window, hermind drifted back to the darkness.

"Please, Miss Cat, I'm scared," seven-year-old Ebony begged. The big, red, Della Reese looking bitch in a bad wig dragged her by her short, nappy hair across the room.

"You dirty, black bitch, I don't give a fuck! You gonna learn to mind what I say!"

"But I did the dishes!"

"Well, you ain't do 'em fast enough," Miss Cat huffed. She grabbed Ebony by her frail little arm as she flung open the closet door with her other hand.

"No, Miss Cat, please! Just beat me! Beat me!" Ebony cried, trying to pull away.

She knew Ebony was terrified of the dark, but she got a sick sense of pleasure making Ebony suffer alone.

Smack!

She smacked Ebony so hard, the room seemed to tilt.

"Don't sass me, bitch! Get yo' ass in there! I'm tired of lookin' at yo' ugly black ass!" Miss Cat ranted.

She threw Ebony into the closet, causing her to get her feet tangled up in the clothes on the floor and falling, hitting her head against the wall. She crumpled in the corner on top of an old suitcase.

Clunk!

That sound was the worst sound in the world. The all too familiar sound of Miss Cat locking the door. It meant, not only wasshe lost in the dark, but she couldn't get out.

To her young mind, she didn't know which was worse.

The scurrying noise in the corner froze her in place. Rats. They lived in the walls, and the closet was one of their entrances into the house. She was scared. Warm pee drizzled down her legs.

"Please, please God, don't leave me in here," she prayed over and over and over, until over the years, her prayers became, "Please God, just let me die." And when there was no answer even for that, she simply stopped praying, thinking God himself had abandoned her as well. The only thing she could count on to be with her was her fear and shame. Shame, as she thought of how the kids at school would pick on her unmercifully. Calling her black monkey, black booga bitch, dirty, ugly, stinking. But they didn'tlive with a woman who refused to wash her clothes. They didn'tlive with a woman who made them eat cat food while the cats ate their food. Ebony came to see herself through the eyes of her tormentors, and all she wanted was to die.

But that was then.

Now, standing at that motel window, the smell of her first kill was still fresh in her nose, and all she wanted to do was kill again and again.

"Before we leave town, we've got one more stop to make. I need a gun," she told Bless, and she couldn't wait to even thescore.

CHAPTER NINE

11:07 a.m.

The small upscale boutique even smelled like money. As soon as Bless and Ebony walked in, their feet sank six inches because of the thick beige carpet. A symphony orchestra played at a comfortable level in the background. Thestore was empty except for a statuesque blonde, who looked like she could've been a runaway model twenty years ago. She came from behind the counter.

"Umm, excuse me, can I help you?" the woman asked. Her tone balanced between polite approach and cold disregard.

Ebony and Bless looked at each other, but mentally shrugged it off.

"Yeah, do you have the latest Stuart Weitzman line?" Bless inquired.

"We do," the blonde replied, subtly looking them up and down. "But you do realize they cost well over two thousand dollars, don'tyou?"

Bless chuckled to bite back the mounting frustration.

Ebony cut in. "It's Valentine's Day. We want to splurge alittle."

"Yes, I'm sure," the blonde said, with an obvious contempt. "Look, is there a problem? I mean, it ain't like we ain't got dough," Bless spat, pulling out a wad of money. It was speckled with blood, but the woman didn't notice.

"Right this way," she replied, subtly rolling her eyes.

As Bless and Ebony walked behind her, Bless reached for his waist, but Ebony stopped him.

"Baby, relax. If it's that serious, let's just go," she whispered.

Bless took a deep breath. One look at Ebony's smile, and he remembered why they were there. He promised to make the day about her.

"I'm good, yo," he replied, gritting his teeth.

They reached the back wall, which was covered with beautiful and most stunning shoes on display. The blonde turned to them and said, "As you can see, we have many varieties to choose from."

Ebony stood wide-eyed with amazement—like a kid in a candy store. Everything looked edible! Just gazing at the display made her feel special, because no one had ever done anything evenremotely as nice as this for her.

"Baby, are you sure?" Ebony inquired.

Bless held up two wads of money. "Shop 'til you drop." He smiled.

The blonde cleared her throat and checked her watch like they were wasting her time. "So which would you like to buy?"

Every shoe looked stunning. She wanted them all, so of courseit was hard for Ebony to decide.

"Let me see . . . can I try this one and this one . . . and this one,"she said, picking out three pairs and holding them out to the blonde. "In a size six, please."

"Ummm, I'm sorry, but we don't allow the customer to actuallytry on the shoe. You have to buy it."

"Don't allow?" Bless echoed, his vexation obvious. "What the fuck kinda shit is that?"

The blonde bristled. "Sir, you don't have to use that type of language. Our policy is—"

"Would that be your policy if we were white?" he wanted to know.

"Bless, baby, it's okay. I didn't really like this boutique anyway. Let's just go somewhere else," Ebony suggested.

Bless looked at her, and the glumness on her face damn near brought tears to his eyes. It was like somewhere deep inside she expected to be treated so disrespectfully. That's when Bless lost it.

"Yo, check this out," he said, slowly licking his lips and subtly biting the bottom one for emphasis. "Take your white ass back there and bring out a size six of everything in the goddamn store before I break your goddamn jaw!"

The blonde snapped to attention. "That's it! You will not talk to me like that! I'm calling the police!" she announced, glad that he gave her a reason to.

Bless snatched her by her hair, wrapped it around his hand, then used it to turn her face to his. He punched the bitch with such force, the crack of her jaw breaking sounded like someone stepping on a tree branch. *Thwack!*

"Bless, noooo!" Ebony bellowed.

"No, please!" the woman mumbled, her mouth filled with so much blood, that if she swallowed she would've drowned.

Bless pulverized her face with a succession of blows that knocked her out, only to be awakened by the next one. When he finally let her go, her body dropped to the floor like a sack of potatoes. Her face looked like the bloody pulp of rotten tomatoes. Bless stood over her, chest heaving.

Ebony grabbed his arm. "Please, Bless, let's go! We're in enough trouble already," she begged.

"Fuck that, yo. I don't give a fuck! This bitch disrespected you, and I swear on everything I am, nobody will ever treat you like thatagain!" he raged.

The sentiment brought tears to her eyes. That was the second time Bless had shed blood over her, and she couldn't lie, she liked it. Watching him beat his own partners with a bat over her, then watching him beat the woman, released something dark inside. A spark that deep down cried out, "Kill them! Yes! Yes! Kill 'em!"

The blood had her transfixed. She was completely mesmerized by it; her whole body trembled. Her pussy even twitched andmoistened.

Bless swiped a can of Lysol off a table behind the counter and snatched a lighter from his pocket.

"So you don't like black people, huh? I wonder how you gonna feel when you blacker than my black ass!" he spat, laughing wickedly.

He flicked the lighter and pressed the nozzle of the Lysol behind it.

Whooooooooosh!

"Oh my—" Ebony started to say. She wanted to turn away, butthe dark side of her wouldn't allow it.

The blonde came to just enough to recognize what washappening.

"Eeeeeeee!" she screeched as soon as the heat got near her face. The flame ate her pale white skin, and it crackled like pork skins. She tried to pop up. Bless placed his foot on her chest, pinning her to the floor as he bent over.

Whooooooooosh!

The second time he flamed her face, the pain was so intense, that more pain had no way of registering. All her body did was twitch several times as he turned her face into a human barbecue. The stench smelled like leather and rotten flesh burning. By the time he finished, her face looked like a burnt marshmallow, black and crisp, with white pus oozing through the cracks.

Bless slowly stood up. "Now . . . try your shoes on," he said quietly, handing her the lighter.

She tucked it in her purse. "What about—"

"Try 'em on!" The harshness in his voice caused her to jump and head straight for the back.

She pulled down the boxes of size six after six, not finding the particular shoes she picked out, but having a ball trying on each and every pair of the sexy heels.

Bless stood in the door and watched her, smiling like a proud father. Seeing her full of excitement was worth the moment. He decided right then, if they were going out, they were going out in style.

"I like those. They make your calves look sexy as hell."

She looked down at the green crocodile-skin Jimmy Choo stiletto with the five-inch dagger heel. She playfully struck a pose.

"You like what you see, huh?"

"I wanna fuck the shit out of you wearin' nothin but them." Bless licked his lips.

"You know I'm down for whateva. But Bae, I don't knowwhich ones I like best."

"Ma, the store is yours. Take 'em all!"

They both laughed, exhilarated by their own power. Bless wrapped his arms around her, kissed her nose and said, "Youbeautiful, you know that?"

"You make me feel that way," she answered, looking him in theeyes, then added, "Bless, how does it feel to kill somebody?"

He smiled then answered, "It's better than sex." His answer further sparked her curiosity.

She settled on three pairs of Stuart Weitzman's and the Jimmy Choos. Bless hit the register and pocketed the money. On the way out the door, they looked back at the dead burnt sales lady.

"It's a shame how they treat niggas." They both laughed and walked out.

"Where to now?" Ebony asked once they got in the car. "You'll see."

They drove to a jewelry store and Ebony looked at him. "What are we doing here, Bless?"

"Come on yo! What's Valentine's Day without diamonds?"

CHAPTER TEN

10:16 a.m.

Why you wanna bring me here?" Bless questioned with ahint of skepticism.

"Because, I know no one will look for you here," Ebony replied as she locked the door.

Bless looked at her as if he could figure her out with one glance. "Why would you help me, after I . . ." his voice trailed off, not wanting to speak the unspeakable.

Ebony didn't answer. She allowed her gaze to brush across his as she turned away. "Do you want me to take a look at that?" she asked.

He looked down at his bloody shoulder. His shirt was already beginning to stick to the wound.

"It'll be a'ight."

"It could get infected, and I know you ain't tryin' to go to the doctor," she reminded him.

"So what? You a doctor now?"

Ebony let her first smile play subtly across her lips. "Just take off your shirt."

Bless sat on the edge of the brown leather sofa and tried to lift his shirt over his head, but his shoulder was throbbing with pain. "Shit!" he cursed, pulling his arms down.

"See? Your arm is about to fall off already," Ebony kidded.

She helped him pull his shirt off. His scent made her weak in the knees. She could smell herself on him under the blood and sweat. She squeezed her thighs together in an attempt to calm the throb.

"I-I'll be right back," she stammered, slightly blushing as she backed away.

Ebony went into her bathroom, opened the medicine chest, took out the alcohol and peroxide. Then she grabbed a towel and wash cloth. When she closed the cabinet, she looked at herself in the mirror. Her usual sour expression was gone. The dull glaze over her brown eyes had seemed to clear up like sunshine after a cloudy day. Her face actually had a slight glow, and her dark chocolate complexion seemed to shine. When she thought about why, she felt herself blush.

Get it together, girl, her reflection told her. She stood there for a few more minutes trying to clear her head.

She took a deep breath, then returned to the living room to find Bless sitting on the sofa with his head in his hands, not wanting to believe what just happened. She had no idea that he was trying to figure out what to do *with* or *to* her.

She admired the way his back vee'd like a cobra's head, the result of hundreds of pull-ups out on the prison yard.

He felt her presence and looked up at her. "*The Butler, Twelve Years A Slave, The Color Purple*? So depressing.

Where's *Act Like A Lady Think Like A Man* or *The Best Man*? Then he pointed to the CDs. "Leela James, Vivian Green, Jill Scott? You strikin' out, ma. I'm sayin', where is Kanye, Pac, Nas and Jay?" Bless questioned.

"You want me to do this or not?" Ebony teased, trying to mask her anxiety with sass, like a little girl with a crush playing grown up.

Bless moved to the arm of the sofa, fighting the pain. Ebony stood between his legs while she gently cleaned his wound.

"Are you sure you didn't get shot?" she asked, trying to inspect his arm. It had a long, deep gash, and she wasn't sure what a bullet wound looked like.

"Nah. It happened when we went through the window," heanswered.

As she worked, her eyes wandered over his body. From his broad shoulders to his hard, sculpted chest, to his rippled six-pack. She had an overwhelming urge to run her tongue over each ripple, down, down, down, until . . .

His words broke her out of her fantasy. "You know I killed a cop, right?"

She nodded, avoiding eye contact, holding her breath, scared if she inhaled his scent . . . their scent, she would no longer be in control of herself. Being so close to him was intoxicating enough.

"When they come for me, they ain't gonna be playin' games," he told her.

"I know," she replied, putting alcohol on the cloth.

"So why didn't you leave when you had the chance?" he questioned.

She put the alcohol-soaked cloth on his wound. He

sucked inhis breath from the sting. Ebony looked him dead in the eyes, then replied, "And go where? This one day has given me more excitement than I've had in my entire life. Plus, I have to admit there's something about you. I'm drawn to you like a magnet. It's- it's . . . crazy to me."

The next few minutes, while she finished up on his shoulder, both of them remained silent, contemplating the crazy destiny their decisions created. She patted his shoulder dry, then handed him a towel.

"I'm going to take a shower. You're welcome to stay until you figure out what you're going to do next," she said, then turned and headed for the back.

She then added, "I'm not old school, but *Reasonable Doubt* is already in the mp3 player."

He smiled, stood up, still fighting the pain and went back over to where the music was.

As soon as Ebony stepped into the shower, she heard the thump of Jay-Z's "Can't Knock the Hustle" rumbling from the living room. She sang the lyrics, giving them a meaning that reflected thereality of her own life.

Bless had kicked open the door of her life, and truth be told, was slowly forcing his way into her heart. It was a strange feeling, one that she knew wouldn't end well, but she truly believed would be worth the ride. All her life she longed to die, but he made her want to live forever. Ebony half expected him to be gone when she came out, never to be seen or heard from again, except each time she closed her eyes she wondered how it would be if he stayed.

She had been so wrapped up in her own thoughts, she hadn't heard him push open the door, didn't hear him pull back the shower curtain, didn't see him pause for a moment to devour her wet, naked body, chocolate chip nipples erect from thoughts of him, before he reached out and ran his thumb over one of them.

Her breath caught in her throat as she turned and saw him there, standing totally naked, his hard dick rubbing against her thigh.

"Those are big scars on your chest. What happened, Bless?""I got shot when I was younger."

Ebony gasped. "You got shot twice? Or two separate times?

What happened?"

"I stabbed somebody, but it was self-defense. I was a youngin'. Bae, enough about me. I can't keep my hands off of you, girl!" he admitted, like the confession was being ripped from his tongue by his lust.

This time she was the aggressor.

Ebony pulled him to her and sucked on his bottom lip, before she forced her tongue into his mouth, loving the taste of him. She gripped his dick with the other hand, squeezing and pumping it until pre-cum oozed from the tip.

"Why didn't you leave?" she asked, running her tongue over hisearlobe.

"And go where?" he shot back, letting her know he was locked in for the ride as well.

Ebony slowly sank to her knees, savoring every inch of his body along the way. She ran her tongue over each ripple of his six- pack, down, down, down until his dick slapped against her cheek. She rubbed it over her lips before taking the large bell head intoher mouth.

"Sssssssss, you feel good," Bless grunted.

His words encouraged her to take more of him, inch by

inch. Each time she bobbed back to the head, never taking the head out of her mouth, until she had as much of him as she could take. She sucked his dick while she fondled his balls, then ran her tongue along the shaft and slurped them.

Bless was almost ready to explode. He pulled her to her feet. As he lifted her, she anxiously wrapped her legs around his waist. His dick effortlessly found her waiting, wet pussy. She was still sore from earlier, but she welcomed the pain that was wrapped in pleasure.

"Oh fuck! This dick is sooooo good. Make me feel it, daddy.

Make me take it . . . allllll," Ebony sang lustfully.

Bless held her up by her ass, pinning her between the wall and his hard body. He spread her pussy with his fingertips then began to pound, pound, pound her pussy relentlessly, giving her, her wish, even as she clawed his back viciously.

"Ohhhhh fuck, Bless! I want to cum on this dick. Can I cum on your dick, baby? Please!" she moaned.

"Cum for me, Ebony. This your dick now. You can cum all overit!"

She wrapped her legs tighter and bounced on his dick like a pogo stick, every stroke hitting her spot, threatening to send her over the edge. When she came, she sat all the way down on him and Bless exploded right along with her.

"I love you," she gasped, the words coming out for the first time as easy as breathing. She hadn't planned on saying it, at least not out loud. She gazed at him boldly, as if daring him to deny her.

"Ma, I loved you the moment I laid eyes on you. Why you thinkI snatched you up?" he answered.

Ebony erupted with laughter. Not so much from what he said, but relief from the tension of being vulnerable. Like leaping off a cliff into the rays of the sun, then realizing the rays are as strong as arms to hold you up. She covered his face with kisses and held him tight. "Swear you'll take me with you, no matter where you go and no matter how it ends. Can you promise me that?" Ebony demanded.

"I do," he promised her. Realizing the words sounded like a marriage vow.

They dried each other off, then went into Ebony's bedroom. She sat on the bed and began rubbing lotion all over her body. Bless glanced around the room. All the windows were closed and the drapes were drawn tight. He felt boxed in.

"Damn, ma, it's like you living in a big ass closet. You like it dark like this?" Bless asked.

Ebony froze when he mentioned the word closet. "I-I just like it dark," she mumbled.

Bless opened the curtains. She wanted to protest, but held back. The sun rushed into the room like water from a faucet, covering the floor and splashing up against the walls.

"Let the sun kiss that pretty black ass." He chuckled.

"I thought that was your job." She tossed her towel at him and he caught it.

"Think it ain't? Come here, let me kiss it," he teased, diving on top of her and kissing her all over.

"Stop!" she whined, loving the affection and attention.

They rolled back and forth until he lay on top of her, looking into her eyes. "Your eyes slant like a cats. I bet it's a panther in you somewhere."

She let the thought sink in. Ebony couldn't deny it, because there were times when she could hear the growl within, especially now, after being around Bless. She could feel it inside, clawing at the bars of its cage.

His dick stiffened against her again.

"Oh no, no, no! Get up, Bless. We have to figure out our next move," she protested, even though she would've loved nothing more than to guide him inside of her again and make love to him for all of eternity. He reluctantly rolled over.

"Yeah, you right. We gotta get a whip."

"And you some clothes. You can't wear that bloody shirt. We can go to Walmart and grab—"

"Whoa, whoa, Walmart? Where they do that at?" He chuckled.

She finished lotioning her body, then pulled on a pair of boy shorts, giggling. "Well, when you live on a budget, you have to do the Walmart thing sometimes!"

Bless looked around the room. If he didn't know it was her room, he would've never known it was a woman's room. There was nothing feminine about it. No pastels, no soft, seductive colors. Everything seemed to be flat and colorless, and when there was color, it was accidental. The label of her deodorant or the *Vogue* magazine on the dresser. Bless picked it up and flipped through the pages.

"I mean, can't you ball on a budget a little bit? Don't you ever say fuck it and treat yourself to somethin'?" he questioned.

"Nope. I mean . . . I-I don't know. I-I-I guess," Ebony stuttered. She was thinking of the times when she bought the gourmet chocolates because her period had her craving the richest chocolateshe could find. Or the nine-inch dildo with the clit tickler becauseshe was so tired of letting her fingers do the talking. But anything more, to her was useless, especially when it came to clothes. She had no one to dress up for, no one to entice, never feeling enticing, never feeling . . .

"No," she finally said.

"What about these?" he asked, holding out the magazine folded to a page featuring a pair of Stuart Weitzman's heels.

She looked at them, longing, amazed that he picked them outbecause they were the very pair that she liked the most.

"Those pretty little toes would look scrumptious in them rightdere'." Bless grinned as he placed her foot onto his lap.

Ebony set the magazine aside, sighing. "Those are only fordreams. Not me."

Bless kissed her on the neck. "Ma, to me you are a dream. Adream come true."

Her heart fluttered like a caged bird ready to sing. "I love youfor saying that to me, Bless."

"Then let me take you shoppin'." He beamed.

"What?" She giggled, unable to believe her ears. "How we gonna go shoppin' and you are America's most wanted?"

Bless laughed. "I'm the gingerbread man. Later for them. Thisday is all about you. Happy Valentine's Day!"

"Its my birthday!"

"No it's not!"

"Yes it is, Bless. I'm serious."

"Well damn. I really gotta take you shopping. Happy Ebony day!"

"Really Bless? That is so corny! But talk like that makes me want to do nasty things to you," she purred in his ear, grabbing his half erect thug muscle.

"So tell me. In those dreams of yours, what store do you walk into first?"

Ebony thought for a minute, then said, "Well, there is this ritzy shoe boutique downtown . . ."

CHAPTER ELEVEN

9:53 a.m.

It was a split second decision. She had no time to assess, to think, or plan. It was one of those moments when life's course was unalterably altered.

"Come on!" Bless yelled out as the bullets started to fly.

Her mind screamed, *NO! I don't have to!* If her mind had its way, she would've snatched away, lay on the floor and screamed, "Don't shoot! I'm not with him!" But in her heart, there was never a doubt. She took his hand before he even fully extended it.

Boom!

The police kicked the door in.

"Freeze! Freeze! Don't you fuckin' move!" The officer threatened.

They were already ducking into a side room in the small apartment. The window had a fire escape, but Bless had no time to open it.

Instead, he opened it with his body.

Boosh!

He dove through the window like a football player turned torpedo, the glass cutting through his shoulder like a razor, but the adrenaline was pumping too fast for him to feel it. Ebony was right behind him. He pulled her the rest of the way through, just as the police slammed through the door.

Boc! Boc!

Boc! Boc! Boc! Boc!

The police let loose two shots and Bless answered with four. It was just enough to keep any of them from sticking their heads out and getting a clear shot at them. By the time they were turning the corner to the next fire escape landing, a cop came through the window.

"They're going down! Cut off the alley, cut off the fuckin' alley!" the cop yelled into his radio.

Boc! Boc!

He let off two shots out of frustration because he knew the metal would protect them from the gunfire from above.

"Run, ma, run!" Bless shouted. "I am!" Ebony hollered.

Their legs were pumping like pistons as they descended the fire escape. She stumbled. But kept going. When they got to the bottom, they were still a flight up from the ground. Bless didn't hesitate. He grabbed the rail and hopped over it like it was a turnstile. He landed like a cat, on the balls of his feet, then looked up.

"Ebony, jump! I'll catch you!"

Again, no hesitation. Later, she would wonder why she trusted this man so easily after the brutal way they met.

She jumped.

He caught her before her feet even touched the ground.

A policecruiser fishtailed into the alley.

Boc! Boc! Boc!

Bless let off three more shots, then they sprinted in the opposite direction through a door and down some steps. They entered a darkboiler room, her feet slapping cold, wet concrete, splashing through puddles that felt too thick and gooey to be water alone. Rats shrieked. Police sirens could be heard in the distance. The sounds of his and her breathing whispered in her ears. Lungs burning, not knowing how much further she could go.

He read her mind. "We almost there, baby. I got you!" hevowed.

His words were her second wind.

They burst out into a vacant lot and cut onto the streets. Another cop in the opposite direction raced toward them. They sprinted the other way. A man on a sleek midnight Honda VFR 1200F motorcycle sat at the light. Bless didn't ask questions—just ran up on the man, put the gun to his chest, and shot a hole in it that blew his heart out his back. He was on the bike before the man's body was dead on the ground. Ebony hopped on, sirens sounding off in every direction.

"Hold on!" he told her.

But she had been holding on the whole time, so the bike ride would be no different. He leaned down low and she laid her head on his back, swore she could hear his heartbeat. She wrapped her arms around him.

Vrrrrrrrrrrrrrroom!

Smoke was the only thing the police caught as Bless went from zero to eighty in less than a blink. He couldn't help laughing in the wind because he had been riding bikes since he could walk and wheelied to prove it. One wheel leaned back, ninety plus, with Bless changing gears mid-air. He was playing with them now. Ebony laughed with him. It was the freest she'd ever felt. He slowed to a rumbling stop. When he set the bike down, the police were a memory. A distant memory.

"We gotta get somewhere before they bring out the chopper," Bless concluded. He knew he couldn't go to his crib. It was probably already swarming with police.

"Go to my apartment," she suggested.

He hadn't expected a response. He had only been thinking out loud. He glanced over his shoulder at her. "You sure?"

"You have a better idea?" she shot back, an ever so slight sassysmirk coloring her expression.

Oh, shit. Let me find out Shorty feelin' me. Bless was surprisedat her idea. "Lead the way."

CHAPTER TWELVE

9:40 a.m.

"What are you going to do with me?" Ebony questioned, with a hint of fear in her tone.

Bless stopped the stolen vehicle at the light and looked over at her like she was aggravating him.

"Look yo, if you ask me that one more time, what I do to you, you ain't gonna like!" he warned, his gun resting in his lap like a hungry pit bull itching to bark and bite.

"I'm gonna lose my job if I'm not at work by ten. Do you know how hard it is to find a job in this city? If I lose it you might as well just kill me," Ebony huffed, folding her arms over her pert breasts.

Before he could reply, a police cruiser pulled up on Ebony's side of the car. Bless tensed. He shot Ebony a scowl.

"Don't even think about it," he warned, as he wrapped hisfinger around the trigger.

Ebony kept her eyes forward. The cop in the driver's seat glanced over. Bless glanced back and nodded. He knew all the paperwork was in order on the car, all except the fact that the owner was now dead. But that was a fact the police couldn't have known. The cop nodded back. The light turned green. They pulled off. Bless made a left but kept checking the rearview for a coupleof blocks.

"What would you have done if I woulda started screamin' my head off back there?" Ebony probed.

"Shot you," Bless replied flatly.

She smiled to herself because she knew he was lying. She couldfeel it. He didn't save her from them clowns for nothing. Now, she knew exactly what he was going to do with her. He wanted her for himself.

They pulled up to an apartment building and parked across the street. Bless reached in the backseat and retrieved the duffle bag. He then clipped up his other gun and tucked them both on his waist. Ebony watched his every move.

"Once I make this drop, I'll take you to work, a'ight? So be good, and everything goes smooth, ya heard?"

"What if I say no?" she challenged, thinking that now she could test her limits. But his expression appeared lethal, so she knew she was through testing.

"Get out the goddamn car. Shut the fuck up and walk!" Bless spat.

She did as she was told.

When Bless rounded the car, he grabbed her by the arm and yanked her.

****

"Who's the chick?" one of the detectives on

surveillance asked. He and his partner were sitting in their unmarked vehicle up the block, watching their every move.

"I don't know, but she don't look too happy," his partner answered.

The detective shrugged. "Lovers' quarrel. You know these people. They're either fuckin' like jack rabbits or fighting like cats and dogs," he remarked, then said over the radio, "We've got two comin' up. The top dog and some broad. No sign of his partners."

"Ten-four," came the crackled reply.

******

Bless and Ebony walked up the stairs in silence. The only soundwas the gritty shuffle of their shoes on the grimy steps.

Finally, Ebony broke the silence. "Thank you."

Bless glanced at her as they reached the third floor. "You'rethanking me?"

"For stopping your friends from . . . you know," she stuttered.He looked away. "They weren't my friends."

"Well, thank you anyway.""Whateva!" he grunted.

His nonchalant attitude got under her skin. It had taken a lot forher to express her gratitude, so for him to dismiss her so flippantly

. . .

"Do you always have to act so fuckin' hard?" she raged as theyneared the apartment door.

Bless looked at her coldly. "It ain't actin'," he answered,knocking on the door.

"Pssht, please. You ain't give me chocolate for

nothing," Ebonysassed.

"Payment," Bless shot back, suppressing his smirk.

She was so hot she wanted to smack the shit out of him.

"Fuck you!" Ebony spat, just as a tall Puerto Rican opened the door. The Puerto Rican dude chuckled and held up his hands in mock surrender.

"Whoa! Innocent bystander here, hold your fire," he joked.

"It's nothin'," Bless grumbled, yanking Ebony through thedoor.

Ebony snatched away as they walked inside. "Get off me!" shesnapped, her temper blazing.

When the Puerto Rican shut the door and turned to them, heranger dissolved into curiosity. Where do I know him from?

He and Bless shook hands. "What up, Bless?"

"I'm good, Q. How you?"

"You know how I do. On my grind, my nigga, on my grind. Come on and have a seat. Is that what I think it is?" Q asked, referring to the duffle bag Bless was carrying.

Bless and Ebony sat on the couch. Out the corner of his eye, he glimpsed Ebony focusing intently on Q and he felt a tinge of jealously that quickly morphed into attitude.

"Fuck else would it be?" Bless grunted.

"That's what I like about you, Bless. All business." Q winked atEbony.

While they talked, something in Ebony's gut told her she had to place this face. She knew she knew him, had seen him somewhere . . .

Recently.

"So where's JT?" Q inquired.

Dead. Bless thought, but answered, "What does it matter? I'm here. The shit is here. Where the fuck is the money?"

Cop! Ebony's mind screamed so loud, the two men heard it in her jump. She snapped to suddenly, her jerky movements drawing their attention.

"The hell is wrong with you?" Bless scowled. "Nothing," she replied.

Should I tell him? she asked herself, because it was obvious that this was an illegal transaction. Her head said, No! Let it go down. As a matter of fact, tell the cop you've been kidnapped! Save yourself! Get away from his crazy ass!

"No!" she said to herself.

The objection wasn't loud. It wasn't heard, it was simply felt deep down. No. She couldn't allow something to happen to Bless. After all he had done, he had awakened something in her that she didn't even know existed.

If it weren't for him, you'd be dead right now, her heart reasoned.

So the fuck what? That's what we decided, right? Fuck this life!

her mind ranted. Ain't that what you want? To die?

Not anymore, fuck that life! She had found a new one . . . she hoped.

"Where do I know you from?" she blurted out, cutting into their conversation.

Q had pulled out a shopping bag containing several stacks of money. He stopped mid count. "Excuse me?"

"I—I-I know you," Ebony stammered. Then she glanced at Bless. "I know him."

Bless looked at her strangely.

******

"What the hell is going on? What did she say?" the engineer two apartments down asked. He was listening to every word because the apartment was wired. Police were ready to rush in at a moment's notice.

"I don't know? Who is she?" another detective asked.

******

Q looked at Ebony. "I don't think so, but nice to see you anyway," he replied, returning to the count.

"No," she said, more firmly. "Bless, I know him."

"And?" Bless asked, irritated. "What the hell that got to do with—"

"He's a cop!" Ebony spat, scared and relieved at the same time. "He was a part of that raid we had in our building. I remember him."

The whole room froze. Bless looked at Q. Q looked at Bless. Q's eyes looked as if sheets had been snatched off, and he stood totally exposed.

That look was all Bless needed to see.

******

"He's been made!" the engineer screamed.

The detective in the unmarked car out front threw open the car door while simultaneously barking into his radio, "All units move in! Move in! Hugo has been made!"

******

Bless reached first, but Q wasn't far behind. Unfortunately forQ he was still too late.

Boc! Boc! Boc!

Bless hit him three times, once in the neck, twice in the face. They were sitting so close, it was almost point blank. Blood splattered from his exploding face and showered Bless. His wiry frame damn near flipped over the couch. Bless grabbed the shopping bag and stuffed it in his pants and then he jumped up.

"Let's go!"

Let him go! her mind cried out. *You freed him, now free yourself!*

But the conversation playing around in her head was useless. Because in the midst of all the madness, the police gathered like a storm bursting through the door, firing the first shots. When Bless reached out his hand and yelled out, "Come on!" Their eyes met, and the bond that was born would be the strongest either of them would ever know.

CHAPTER THIRTEEN

8:58 a.m.

"Shut up, bitch! You think I'm playin' with you, huh!" JTroared.

Smack!

The slap turned Ebony's head and bloodied her face.

Bless looked away, not knowing why. Something about the girl had gripped him and wouldn't let go. It wasn't like she was a heart-stopping dime. First off, she was black, jet-black. Almost African-black with a short, nappy cut that reminded him of Solange when she was on her weird shit. Her lips and slanted eyes gave her a cat-like femininity, a sex appeal that struck him like the seductive rhythm of a voodoo priestess. Her body was petite and shapely. Her ass wasn't big, because he was able to tell when JT and Pop snatched her out of the car and dragged her inside JT's apartment.

"Please! Why are you doing this?" she cried out.

JT slung her on the couch. Her shoe flew off, revealing a small delicate foot, her toenails painted orange. Bless loved the way the color set off against her dark skin.

Pop stood over her, his huge stomach hanging over his belt. He looked like a thugged-out Anthony Anderson.

"What we gonna do wit' this bitch, Bless?" Pop questioned, sick ideas already dancing in his head.

"Naw, it's what we shoulda been did," JT spat, looking at her with disgust. Then adding, "Ol' ugly black bitch. We shoulda killed her in the store wit' the other muhfuckas!" JT was definitely the psycho in the crew. Standing only five foot four inches and bearing a rare striking resemblance to Prodigy from Mobb Deep, his frailness always made him feel like he had something to prove.

Bless glared at him. "Stupid muhfucka! You shouldn't have killed them! Fuck was you thinkin'?"

Even though JT somewhat feared Bless, he always used bravado to mask it. "Nigga, fuck that! You wasn't talkin' 'bout shit! I did what I had to do!"

"Please, no!" Her shrill cry caught both JT and Bless by surprise. Pop had her pinned down on the couch, her pants and panties around her thighs. They both had their hands on her pants in a tug of war, her pussy being the prize.

"Pop, what the fuck you doin'!" Bless barked.

"Fuck you think I'm doin'? This free pussy!" the fat nigga huffed.

JT laughed, and his laughter grated on Bless's nerves like nails on a chalkboard.

"Fuck it! Might as well have some fun. Shit, she do got some thick-ass thighs. I got next, nigga!" JT ran over and yanked at Ebony's hands to let go of her jeans.

When she didn't he backhanded her, drawing blood

from her mouth. "Bitch, let go! I'm about to fuck the shit outta you!"

"Oh God, help me!" she yelled hysterically as Pop snatched her jeans off so hard, he pulled her onto the floor. JT snatched off the boy shorts in one slick move, leaving them twisted around one of her ankles. He tossed the shorts to the side and feasted his eyes on her clean-shaven pussy. Her dark skin made the pink inner folds of her pussy lips stand out juicy and bold.

"Oh, hell no, nigga! I'm first! Damn, she got a pretty pussy!" JT exclaimed.

"Fuck you, yo. You better put your dick in her mouth or something," Pop grunted, struggling with his belt, trying to take off his pants.

"Nooooo no! Please, noooo!"

Bless tried to ignore her cries, but he couldn't ignore her eyes. He was turning away when their eyes met, but hers wouldn't let go. Her gaze made him feel like he was the only man in the world that could save her. She looked past his pride and into his soul. At that point, he couldn't deny her.

"Ay yo, chill! Let her go!" he told Pop, just as Pop was trying to force his dick inside her tight pussy.

"Nigga, fuck outta here!" Pop growled like a pit bull when someone was foolish enough to try to take his bowl while it was eating.

Bless went over to him, grabbed his shoulder, and threw him off her. Pop instantly felt a way about being tossed aside with his dick in his hand.

"Mutherfucka, I'll—" he threatened, reaching down for his pants to get his gun out of his back pocket.

Bless wasn't about to let him. He kicked him with all he had, in the nuts. The pain was excruciating. Pop couldn't even cry out. The pain took his breath away and knocked him in the back of his head as if he was having convulsions. He rolled around on the floor, wheezing and holding his nuts.

"Muhfucka, get away from my cousin!" JT boomed, reaching for the pistol in his waist.

Bless didn't give him time to pull it out. He dove on top of JT, tackling him chest high and pinning the gun between them.

Boc!

The gun went off once.

The girl yelped as if she got hit, but it actually went into the floor. But she wasted no time pulling up her shorts and grabbing up her pants. Bless held JT's gun hand by the wrist and hit him with a flurry of lefts with the other. JT went cross-eyed, drunk from the blows. He tried to bring the gun up, but Bless knocked it across the floor. The two of them tussled. In the corner stood JT's baseball bat. Bless caught JT with a hard right that made him loosen his hold on Bless. Bless jumped up and grabbed the bat.

And that was all she wrote.

Splat!

The first blow sounded so sickening, it turned the girl's stomach. But Bless was just beginning. He brought the bat down over and over and over onto JT's head. JT had been dead way before the seventh blow. By the eleventh, his head looked like chewed up raw hamburger meat. By this time, Pop was struggling to sit up. Bless laid him right back out.

Blah!

He hit him dead in the face, breaking Pop's jaw and sending teeth everywhere. He bashed Pop on the side of the head. His eyeball leapt from its socket and dangled by the muscle on his cheek. Blow after blow landed, blood flew all over, sprinkling Bless's hands, face, and clothes. He kept beating Pop because Pop kept twitching. Bless didn't realize the twitching was the involuntary muscle spasms of a mutilated corpse.

"Please . . . please . . . stop. No more!"

He heard her voice, and it was the *only* thing that could've reached him at that moment. Not even his mama could have stopped him. But Ebony's words interrupted the storm as instantly as it began. His chest heaved as she stared down at his gruesome work. Pop was damn near headless.

She began to sob uncontrollably. She was more afraid now than when Pop was about to rape her. Bless wanted to comfort her, but he didn't know how. He felt awkward, because he knew he was the cause and effect. He looked at her, unable to peel his eyes away from her dark, chocolate thighs and fat pussy print pushing through the shorts.

Bless let his body take over.

He moved toward her and sat down beside her. Human nature made her crave comfort even if it was from her tormentor.

"Oh my God!" she gasped, "He-he-he was going to—"

"Shhhhh," Bless broke in, not even wanting the evil spoken

aloud. "It's okay, ma."

She looked up at him. Her eyes liquid and beautiful

up close,the kind that artists paint and poets toast.

"Are . . . are they dead?" she dared to ask.

"It don't matter," he replied, then went to wipe her face and dry away her tears.

He used his thumb, but instead of wiping away the tears, he smeared the blood from his hand on her cheek, making her appear as if she was crying blood. The blood blended against her velvety black skin.

"I'm sorry. I got blood on you," he whispered. Her tears wouldn't stop flowing.

Her breath caught in her chest. He tried to wipe her tears with his fingers, trying to catch them before they ran onto her mouth. His thumb brushed her lip. The moisture made him curse under hisbreath.

"Damn!" His hand went to her chin. He stroked it. "You fuckin'beautiful! You know that?"

No. She didn't know that, and she pulled away, backing onto the floor.

He got down next to her. "I'm not gonna hurt you yo. I swear," he vowed, his hands caressing her taut nipple.

"Please. Stop," she gasped.

Unfortunately, he took her by the back of her neck and forced his tongue into her mouth, stopping her protest. She bit it.

"Aaaahh!" he groaned, but the pain only turned him on. He pinned her to the floor by her neck and forced her legs open with his while he took down his pants.

"You can't . . . do this!"

"Fuck that!" He yanked the shorts down.

His dick was so hard it throbbed. She scratched at his bloody face, leaving red whelps, but once his long, fat dick explodedinside her pussy, she dug into the carpet like a car trying to get traction.

"N–n–n–no," she moaned, only because she felt she was supposed to.

Bless pinned her arms over her head, looked her dead in the face, guilty but unashamed. As he pounded her, their bodies clapping, her head thrashed from side to side, her legs in constant motion like she was trying to back pedal away. But when she looked in his eyes, she couldn't look away. No matter how hard she tried.

Bless had a sick desire to fuck her. The dead bodies that lay close were turning him on all the more. The lack of fear in her was driving him insane. He wanted her to be afraid, but unbeknownstto him, her desire to die wouldn't let her. No matter how bad the situation. The dead bodies that they left at the pharmacy, the attempted rape, and now him fucking the shit out of her, still didn't give her one ounce of fear. And that drove Bless mad.

"Tell me to stop," he grunted, daring her to lie.

"St–st–st," she stuttered, unable to get enough breath to finish the word.

Every stroke left her breathless. She could feel him in her stomach, in her womb, banging her pussy, wet enough that she could finally adjust to his size. She felt so full, she wanted to scream. Instead she dug her heels into the carpet like she was trying to press the brakes.

She, however, exploded. Her back arched involuntarily and no sounds escaped, the feeling was too intense. Her mouth hung open. He stuck his tongue in it, but this time she didn't reject him. Her kiss alone made Bless's whole body tense up, because he knew he was no longer in this alone. He pounded until his body jerked, and he filled her with his seed.

All of Bless's life he dealt with bullshit bitches from the projects. None of them were about shit. He never met a chick like Ebony who was fearless. She didn't even threaten to call the policeor cry. She was the type of girl he used to dream about having.

Silent accusation filled the room as he collapsed on top of her. When he lifted himself into push-up position, their eyes met. Hers didn't flinch when she smacked the shit out of him. Bless didn't flinch when he took it. He expected it.

"I hate you!" she spat as she slapped him again.

This time he buried his face in her neck. She pummeled his shoulders and the back of his head with her fist, his thighs with herheels. Then she violently pushed him.

"Get off of me!" she grunted, giving it all the effort her little body could muster.

Bless relented and got up. She quickly scrambled from under him, then scooted up against the wall, bringing her knees up to her chest, glaring at Bless and watching him intently.

"This is why you kidnapped me, isn't it? You planned for this, not them! That's why you killed them," she spewed.

"I was gonna kill them anyway, yo," Bless replied calmly. Henever trusted Pop and JT.

She started to get up. Bless's eyes followed her, alert. "Whatyou doin'?"

"Getting my fuckin' clothes, you mind?"

She reached for her jeans. He grabbed her wrist. "For what?" he growled like a guard dog awakened.

"What you mean 'for what?' I want to get dressed so I can go!" "You ain't goin' nowhere," he replied, snatching up her jeans, balling them up and tossing them across the room.

"Why not! You got what you wanted, right? Why can't I leave?" she demanded.

"Because you can identify me. So you stayin' until I say you can go."

"What you gonna do with me? Kill me like you did them?" she asked.

He looked her deep in the eyes and replied, "Yeah, if you keep runnin' your goddamn mouth."

She leaped up and lunged at him. "Then do it, muhfucka! Do it! Kill me! I don't give a fuck! I wanna die!" she spat, tears spilling down her cheeks. Ebony tried to punch him, but he easily battedher away and seized her by the neck.

"Shut the fuck up before I slit ya muthafuckin' throat." He was cutting off her air. "Now sit . . . your ass down!" he seethed coldly,finally releasing his grip.

She slid down the wall, gasping desperately for air. "What . . . what are you gonna do with me?"

"Stop askin'."

"I deserve to know." She coughed.

"You'll find out."

He got up and went over to the oversized duffle bag. He pulled out the heart-shaped box of chocolates. The package he went back for. The one she was looking at when he first saw her. He tossed it in her lap.

"Here. You hungry?"

She looked at the box and then up at him. She knew he

wasn't just offering her something to eat. The heart-shaped box represented much more. When she looked in his eyes, she knew she was right. Ebony slung the box across the room.

"I hate chocolate!" she snapped.

"Then why were you lookin' at it in the store?" he questioned, holding back a smirk.

There was a tense pause.

"You don't know nothin' about me." "Not even your name," he added.

Defensive, she folded her arms over her bare breasts. She could still hear him telling her she was beautiful, still feel him inside of her, his rhythm pounding in sync with her heartbeat.

"Can I put on my clothes at least?" "You gonna tell me your name?" "Fuck you."

Silence.

A moment later, he got up, got her pants, her shirt, her shoes and handed them to her. She snatched them out of his hands. Just when he thought he had failed to reach her, failed to convince her with his energy that this was no ordinary love. Just when he was about to say, "Fuck it", she said, "My name is Ebony."

CHAPTER FOURTEEN

8:19 a.m.

E verybody on the fuckin' floor now! You! What you think,it's a game?"

Blah!

Blood flew from the pharmacist's mouth as JT slapped him with the butt of the riot pump. He stumbled and fell against a rack of magazines, bringing it crashing to the ground.

"Move bitch, or you next!" Pop bellowed, putting the gun to theyoung woman's head.

She dropped the heart-shaped box of chocolates she was holding and slowly lowered herself to the floor. Pop pushed her therest of the way down.

Bless noticed she didn't look scared. The pharmacist, a hefty- sized black man and his slim, gay assistant screamed like a couple of bitches as well as the older black woman patron. But the young woman didn't even blink an eye. That was the second thing he noticed.

The first was her beauty.

It wasn't the kind of beauty that hit you in the face and blinded you. Not a Beyoncé, Gabrielle Union, Alicia Keys type beauty.

No.

Her beauty was like a voodoo spell. Once cast, it never let go. Hers was the beauty of the black woman, raw, uncut and pure. Her short, kinky afro, tapered off at her graceful neck. Her silhouette, subtly shapely, and her jet-black frame seemed to have a glow within, like the sun dipped in darkness.

He forced his mind back to the task at hand, then jumped the counter and put the gun to the back of the gay dude's head. He lay on the floor munching the rug.

"Oh, Lord Jesus, please don't shoot!" he exclaimed, sounding like Butterfly from the Steve Harvey morning show.

Bless kicked him in the face. "Shut your bitch ass up! We want the opiates, the liquid opiates, the Benzo's and syringes, ya heard?"

Too scared to speak, the fruit nodded, holding the side of his swelling face.

"I asked if you heard me?"

"Yes, yes, lord yes. Just don't kick me no mo'!" the fruit begged.

Bless snatched him up by the collar of his white coat. He scrambled to his feet. Bless shoved him toward the back, where all the pills were kept and took the empty, oversized duffle bag off his shoulders. He opened it and set it on the floor.

"Fill it up!" he ordered.

The fruit began to dump the large jars of pills and

different colored tablets and capsules into the bag. He carefully laid several jugs of liquid opiates inside as well. In a few minutes he was done.

"That's it?" Bless questioned.

"We-we haven't restocked. We only—"

Boc!

The fruit dropped to the floor, howling, reaching for his right foot that was gushing blood.

"You think I'm playin' wit' yo' faggot ass? The next one is goin' in your head!" Bless threatened. "Now get up and give it up!"

This time the fruit wasted no time giving him everything he asked for. Bless hoisted the bag onto his shoulder.

"Thank you for cooperation." Bless smirked, then leveled thegun right at his face.

"Noooooo!"

Boc! Boc!

Both shots went straight through his eye, blowing the socket as wide as his forehead. His body crumpled to the ground. Bless cameout the back just as Pop was putting the riot pump, point blank to the back of the pharmacist's head.

Boom!

One shot and he was left damn near headless. Pop was rightbehind with his shots, as he turned to grandma.

"Jesus, no!" she screamed.

"Bitch, be happy, 'cause you about to meet him!" Pop laughed.

Boc! Boc! Boc!

He blew her wig off with half her brain attached. The rest began to ooze out once she hit the ground. JT turned the gun toward the young girl.

"No!" Bless blurted before even he realized he had said it. JT scowled. "Fuck you mean '*no*?' We said no witnesses!"

Bless stepped to JT. "Nigga, what I say? This my lick! Playyour position! She's comin' wit' us just in case!"

"In case of what?" Pop wanted to know.

Bless didn't answer. He went over to the girl. "Get up. Let'sgo!"

"I'm not going anywhere!" she answered, refusing to look athim.

He looked at Pop. "Get this bitch up and get her to the car!"Bless ordered.

Pop didn't ask any questions. He snatched her up by the collarand put his gun to her neck.

"Move!"

And she did . . . reluctantly.

Bless started behind them, but he doubled back. "Where you goin'?" JT asked, vexed.

Bless bent down and picked up a package, then he put it in the duffle bag. "Nigga, just go!" No sooner than the word 'go' left his mouth, the police cruiser was coming their way hitting the curb, missing them by inches as it crashed head-on into the front display window.

"What the fuck!" Bless yelled out as they made their getaway.

CHAPTER FIFTEEN

8:12 a.m.

Happy birthday to me," Ebony mumbled as she picked up the heart-shaped chocolate box off the display.

Valentine's Day was the worst day of the year for her because it was also her birthday. It was a yearly reminder that, not only did she not have someone to share it with— she didn't have anyone to call her own. She was totally alone in a world that didn'tgive a damn. She longed to die.

For some time she had resisted the pull that death had on her. It was her constant companion. The only company she could count on.

"Come to me," death would whisper. "I'll embrace you, I'll comfort you. We'll be together forever."

She had fought it for so long, that she could no longer resist.She had come to the pharmacy to buy a bottle of sleeping pills. In her purse was a suicide note addressed to the City Morgue since she didn't have anyone else who cared enough to send it to. That thought alone pushed her over the edge.

"Fuck it!" she mumbled.

She looked at the heart in one hand and the sleeping pills in the other. How she longed to have someone give her a box of candy. Just one sweet gesture that said life was worth living, don't giveup. *Was that too much to ask?*

For the life of her, she didn't know what possessed her to buy the key chain that other day. A feeling inside her that she couldn't describe, one that warmed her but chilled her at the same time.

Jermaine . . .

She thought of him often, wondering if he was okay. Wondering if he had it better or worse than her. Wondering if he had to grow up with HIV and how he handled it. Sometimes she would dream about meeting him, but deep down she knew she wouldn't be able to pick him out of a crowd. She could no longer see his baby face.

Before she knew it, the pharmacy door flung open. She turned her head to see who it was. The flash of the steel took her by surprise, but the man holding that same piece of steel took her breath away.

CHAPTER SIXTEEN

8:08 a.m.

Bless had already outlined his plan to JT. He was casing the pharmacy because he planned on making it his next lick.

His money was getting low, and he could feel his body missing the meds because he kept getting chills and breaking into cold sweats no matter how warm it was.

"Yeah yo, I'm feeling that," JT agreed. "We knock off a pharmacy, and it's bound to be eight, nine thousand pills up in there."

"And we'll get rich!" Pop added.

"You sure your man Q can handle an order like that?" Bless questioned.

"Shit, Q paper long!" JT bragged, not knowing his man G was actually the police.

"Say no more then. I am on it," Bless assured him.

Every morning for a week Bless was there when it opened. He knew exactly what time the manager opened the door, what time a police cruiser was going to be in the area, and when the second employee came in. He also knew when she stepped off the bus.

The first day, he didn't pay her any attention. She came in three days in a row, and on that third morning he saw her face, and knewhe had to have her. Something about her eyes drew him in. He sensed she could see the same things he did, as if she knew the shape of his demons. If she ever noticed him, she never acknowledged him. It made him want to get close to her.

On the fifth day, he violated the code of casing a target by showing his face. But something he couldn't control pulled at him.

He walked right behind her. She even held the door by reaching back and not letting it close.

"Thanks," he told her. "Yeah," she mumbled.

He was tall enough to see over the aisle shelves. He stayed back, but close enough to catch a whiff of her flowery scent and hear her voice when she went to the counter.

"Hey girl, how you doin' today?" the flamboyant cashier asked. "I'm good, Dion. Just another day, you know?"

"Well, it wouldn't be if you smiled more. Let the world see that chocolate shine, and your prince charming will come a-callin'!" hesang playfully.

She snickered, "I know that's right."

Her voice sounded familiar in a strange way to Bless. Like a voice he had heard in his dreams. Somewhere deep down in him it was haunting, but at the same time beautiful. He had seen enough so he dipped out.

Ebony spotted some key chains on the counter, the kind

with people's names on it as she spun the display past the A's, B's, C's, all the way to the J's. She spotted the name she was looking for.

"Add this in, please." The nosy cashier read it.

"Jermaine? Mmm, let me find out," he snickered femininely.

Ebony mustered a smile. "Dion, your mind stays in the gutter. It ain't even like that, thank you."

"Then by all means, do tell. I love juicy stories."

Ebony grabbed her bag off the counter and winked. "Maybe some other time." She walked out the store fingering the key chain.

******

On that eighth day, Bless coughed long and hard, putting JT on alert. He looked in the rearview mirror. "Goddamn, nigga! Don't give me that cold!"

You already got it. Bless kept that thought to himself. He sat in the backseat behind the passenger, Pop, as JT drove them to the pharmacy. In Bless's lap were two .40 caliber pistols. He loaded the clip with his gloved hand, then slid the clip into the butt of one of the .40 calibers.

Click–Clack! Click–Clack!

Both guns were now locked and loaded.

"Yo, this nigga better have the money," Bless remarked, eyeing the back of JT's head.

JT snorted. "Nigga, didn't he have it the last time?" he countered.

Truth be told, JT hadn't done the background check on Q. Bless had been introduced to him by his man, Pete when he got out of county jail. JT was thirsty and didn't even recognize that Pete was a shaky motherfucker from the jump. That's when JT brought the move to Bless as soon as he came home from prison. After checking it out, Bless had agreed that the spot was perfect to hit fora whole lot of pills. At least a fifty-stack lick. Petty cash if split between three people, but Bless had no intention of splitting anything except their heads. Bless was a greedy motherfucker. He wanted it all.

"I'm just sayin' yo, this shit is sweet. I been layin' on this shit for a while. Only two muhfuckas in there—"

Pop cut JT off. "Nigga, you already told us that. How much you think we gonna get?" Pop questioned gluttonously.

Two to the head a piece, Bless thought. But he said, "About fifteen a piece."

"Hell yeah!" Pop cackled, then gave JT a high five. "I'ma ball tonight!"

JT parked across the street from the pharmacy. He looked over the seat at Bless. "You ready?"

Bless smirked wickedly and kissed both pistols. "Am I!" With nothing to lose and ready to die, Bless was turning into a stone- cold killer, who savored every chance he got to prove it.

"Time to prove it, baby boy!" JT said.

Shick–Shack!

JT cocked the riot pump. "Let's make it happen!" he yelled.

They all got out, keeping their guns close. The area was quiet this early in the morning. They kept their heads on swivel. Bless grabbed the door and flung it open. He caught her silhouette out the corner of his eye. He looked. She looked. He may have been stealing the drugs, but she stole his heart first.

You comin' wit' me, he thought, realizing that this wasn't going to be the typical Valentine's Day. Then he yelled, "Thuggz Valentine, muhfuckazzzz!"

THE MIDDLE
JT, Neecie, and Pop

CHAPTER SEVENTEEN

Several days earlier . . .

L et's do this!" JT barked as he pulled the ski mask over his face. Pop and Stank did the same as they ran up on the woman unlocking the door of the check-cashing place.

"Oh my God!" she gasped.

"You betta shut up, bitch!" JT warned, pushing her inside.

She stumbled forward, breaking a heel and falling onto her face. Stank quickly shut the door, something Pop was supposed to do, but he got stuck gawking at the woman because her skirt flapped up, exposing the pretty pink panties underneath.

"Yo, nigga!" JT barked at Pop. The sound of his big cousin's voice brought him back to reality.

"I'm wit' you, fam!" Pop assured him.

"Stay focused!" JT yelled as he snatched the woman by her hair.

"Please don't hurt me!" she begged.

"Then don't give me a reason to," JT advised, sticking thebarrel of his gun right under her chin. "Open the safe!"

"It's time locked! It opens at 9:10!" she explained.

JT glared at Stank through the mask. "Nigga, I thought you said9:05!" he snapped.

"I thought it was 9:05!" Stank replied. JT glanced at the clock on the wall: 9:07.

"Shit!" JT cursed, looking out the window at the cars breezing past. He didn't care about catching bodies, but he hated for a job not to go as planned. Each second ticking by seemed to take an eternity. JT's eyes were glued to the clock.

Stank's eyes stayed on JT, because he knew he had disappointed him. Pop's eyes stayed on the woman. His gaze licked her red painted toes that teasingly peeked at him through herpump. Her legs were thick because she was short and plump. The stockings made him want to rip a hole in them and fuck herthrough them. His dick got hard just thinking about it.

"Nine-ten! Open it now!" JT ordered, shoving her toward the safe door.

Nervously, she attempted to enter the combination. JT smacked the shit out of her. Her knees wobbled, but JT's grip on her hair kept her steady. "Bitch, don't try to play me! Open the safe, or I'ma open your head!"

The woman tried again, concentrating with everything she had because she was terrified of the consequences of screwing upagain.

Click!

The sound of the safe opening was sweeter than a bitch having an orgasm to JT's ears. He shoved the woman out of the way and threw open the door.

"Stank, move! Move! Pop, watch her!" JT ordered as he dashed inside the safe with Stank.

Pop gripped the woman's arm and pulled her next to him. Her heels made her taller than Pop.

"Take off your shoes," he ordered.

She wasted no time in following his instructions. He looked down at her small pedicured toes and licked his lips with desire. "You got some pretty feet," Pop whispered.

The woman, feeling the lust radiating off him, tensed with fright, dreading what she feared he'd do to her. "Pl–please," she sobbed.

Pop's dick hardened. He loved the power he had over women who couldn't put up a struggle. He slid his hand up the back of her skirt. The woman instinctively tried to move away.

"Just take the money. Please leave me alone," she begged, but that only excited him more.

Pop slid his hand inside her panties and squeezed her soft ass. Itjiggled like jelly between his fingers.

"Goddamn you fat!" he lustfully exclaimed, shoving two fingersinside her pussy.

The woman's whole body shook with sobs. "Why are you doingthis?" she cried out.

Pop began vigorously finger-fucking her, but despite her repulsion, her pussy began getting wet. Pop thought it meant she really wanted it.

"Yeah, bitch, I knew you were a freak. Bend over for this dick,"his voice boomed. He bent her over the desk.

JT and Stank moved with the swiftness. JT checked his watch. It only took them two minutes to snatch up all the money. So when he turned and saw the woman bent over the desk, panties pushed to the side and Pop finger-fucking her, he was damn near livid.

"Nigga, fuck kinda shit you into!" JT spazzed.

Pop snatched his fingers out and jumped back. "My bad, cuz.

The bitch beggin' for it," his sick mind reasoned.

JT shook his head and handed him the other bag. *If Pop wasn't fam', I would've been put a bullet through his head.* He smacked the pistol down on the back of the woman's skull, knocking her unconscious.

"Come on!" his voice roared. Then the three of them jetted out the door, money in hand.

******

Stank drove the getaway car. Pop sat in the back and JT rode shotgun. They had gotten back to the hood and were about to switch cars from the stolen sedan.

"Yo, J, man. My bad on the timer. I thought it was earlier," Stank apologized, knowing it was the slip ups that got a nigga fucked.

JT chuckled. "Pull up around back," JT told him, pointing to an abandoned building where his car was parked. "Everybody makes mistakes, you know? Mine was fucking with you."

Without hesitation, JT put the gun to the side of Stank's head and blew his brains all over the driver's side window. Stank's body jerked, and what was left of his face slammed against the window and stuck. He was still driving at the time, so JT had to extend his leg across Stank's and stomp his dead foot on the brake.

"Grab the money," JT told Pop as they both jumped out of the car and headed for JT's Caddy.

As soon as they pulled away, Pop peered into the bags greedily. "How much you think we got?"

"We?" JT smirked. "You better be glad I ain't leave you wit' Stank, wit' your freaky ass."

Pop snickered. "Nigga, you love me too much." "That's my problem."

JT's phone rang. At first he started to ignore it, but when he saw it was Neecie, he answered.

"What up, ma?"

"Where you at?" she questioned. "Right here," he joked. "What's good?"

Neecie sucked her teeth. "Don't play wit' me, JT. I got somethin' for you."

"What?" "Come see."

"Yo, Neecie, I'm into somethin' right—" "Boy, it's about money."

Now she had his attention. "What's good?"

"Bless is home, and he got somethin' I think you'll like."

"He home? When that nigga get out? Why he ain't holla at me?"

"What you think I'm doin'?"

As soon as JT heard Bless's name, old emotions welled up inside him. When Bless was on the street, he was the most feared stick-up kid. Now JT was. So JT felt like he had something to prove. Plus, he knew he would have to face him for fuckin' Neecie, eventually. He figured he might as well get it over with.

"Say no more. I'm on my way." If Bless had a move, he knew it was big. And if it was big enough, JT wouldn't hesitate to leave Bless the same way he left Stank.

CHAPTER EIGHTEEN

BACK TO BLESS . . .

My nigga!" "JT!"

The two old friends greeted each other with boisterous acknowledgment and gangsta hugs, but the smiles didn't quite match the look in their eyes. Both had reason to be wary of the other. JT, because Bless was the dude he aspired to be, and the fact that he had fucked his girl and gave her two sons. And Bless, because he was like the old champ and jealous of the new one. But on the surface, it seemed all good.

"What up, yo? When you get out?" JT asked, giving him the once over and taking in Bless's enhanced physique. "I see you been on that weight pile."

Bless sneered. "Naw yo! Nothin' but pull-ups. Them shits cut a nigga up like a bag of dope. You know what's up. But where Pop at?"

"He at the crib. I just dropped him off. He had to take care of something, but he sends his love, and he say he definitely gonna see you soon," JT told him.

Neecie walked in the room wearing shorts and an oversized basketball jersey that hung on her like a dress. "Nigga, you need to hit me off like you said you would. Your son needs some pampers, and you ain't gave me a dime in damn near two months. These your kids, JT," she huffed like the hood rat she was and got in his face.

JT's smile turned into an upside frown. He shot her a scowl before pushing her back onto the sofa. He wanted to slap the shit out of her, not only for her putting him on the spot in front of

Bless, but it was as if she was trying to shine on him and make him look small and irresponsible. And he knew that she had been waiting for Bless to come home just so she could hop back onto his dick.

"Bitch, shut the fuck up and take yo' ass outside somewhere!" JT spat, his look saying he was one more word off her ass. "Let grown men take care of business." But what he really wanted to say was, "Bitch, what you gonna do when and if this nigga's body end up in a river somewhere or right back in the joint? Whose dick will you be trying to jump on then?"

On the flipside, Neecie, in his mind, proved that he was the champ and now he finally got his chance to stunt on Bless.

How you like me now, nigga?

****

Three hundred grand was the type of lick he had dreamed of hitting while he was locked up. He may not have had long to live, but he planned on enjoying every minute of what was left. Bless nodded as he hit the blunt.

"If the shit was that sweet, why you ain't already take him downyourself?" Bless asked, then passed the blunt to Pop.

JT shrugged. "Simple. We can't get close to Fareed. The nigga live out in the suburbs somewhere and rarely show his face."

"And when he do," Pop added, lying through his teeth, "the muhfucka have more fuckin' shooters around him than the goddamn President."

"Word? He heavy like that? I was only gone for twenty-four months. How he come up like that?" Bless questioned, clearly impressed.

"Fam', the nigga hustles. But trust me. When I say three hundred large, that's worst case scenario. His bitch is a slow leak with a fast tongue, and she get her hair done with a bitch I know," JT explained, handing Bless the blunt he just took from Pop.

Bless inhaled the earth. "So what makes you so sure I can get close to him like that?"

"Man, stop playin', yo. That nigga idolized you." Pop chuckled. "As soon as he find out you home, he gonna be checkin' for you to try to get you on the payroll. Then you'll be in like Flynn."

Shit, I probably won't even be around by next pay cycle, he thought, but said, "Then let's get this paper!" He dapped up JT andPop.

*****

It took about a week before the word made its circuit in the street, and Bless was able to get in touch with Fareed.

When the call came through Bless's cell phone, the number was unknown. He usually didn't take such calls, but since he was anticipating dude, he took the chance.

"Yo," he answered.

"This Bless?" Fareed asked, his voice both nervous and excited at the same time.

"Shit, you already know! What's good, my nigga?" Bless greeted him like he was a long lost buddy.

Bless was greeted by a short silence. "Hello?" Bless said, just to test the line.

"How I know this really Bless? I thought Bless was locked up."

To Bless, the nigga didn't sound like a balla. He sounded like a nigga so paranoid he was hiding under the bed.

"Nigga, I didn't have a life sentence." Bless chuckled. "This bid was only a little over two."

Bless could hear the relief in Fareed's voice. "I just needed to make sure. What up, my nigga? What's good?"

"You, from what I hear."

"What you mean?"

Bless took the comment as a signal that Fareed didn't want to talk on the phone. "Nothin' yo, just kickin' it. But on the real, come scoop a nigga. Let's put our heads together," Bless suggested.

There was a short pause before Fareed replied, "Yo, you ain't heard?"

"Heard what?"

"Nothin'. I just don't be around the way like that no more. But I do wanna see you, my nigga. I might need your help with somethin'," Fareed hinted.

Cha–ching! Went the cash register in Bless's head.

"Say no more, my nigga. Just tell me when and where. You know you can count on me."

"Not today. Tomorrow. Take the train to Jersey City. I'mascoop you from Journal Square."

"Cool. What time?"

"Just be there around twelve. I'll call you."

Click!

Bless looked at the phone as if that was the strangestconversation he ever had, then he called JT.

"Yo, J, it's on, baby!"

******

"Goddamn, where this nigga at?" Bless cursed under his breath as he paced in front of Journal Square. He checked his watch for the umpteenth time: 2:40 p.m.

He was ready to bounce, when a gray Kia Sedona pulled up. Hepeered inside and saw Fareed.

"Come on, my nigga, get in," Fareed told him, peeping in the rearview, looking all around as if he had just taken a blast of crack cocaine.

Bless got in and Fareed pulled off. Once he felt everything wassafe, his whole demeanor lightened up and he gave Bless dap.

"What's good, fam'? Damn, it's good to see you! You alldiesel and shit!" Fareed cracked.

Bless laughed. "Nigga, look at you, fat as a muhfucka. Youeatin' good, huh?"

Fareed chuckled and stroked his thick Rick Ross beard. "That'swhat happens when you get married, yo."

"Married? What the fuck, my nigga?""Don't worry, you about to meet her."

Bless wasn't surprised to see Fareed head right back to Newark. *Shit, if a nigga go through all that bullshit, Newark to Jersey City and back to Newark again, he gots to be caked up!* Bless thought, then sat back and enjoyed the ride.

They arrived in a section of Newark called Vailsburg, a sleepy little township, which was still the hood. He was right under their nose.

Smart, Bless concluded. *But I still ain't convinced that he ballin' the way JT said he was.*

Fareed moved with relaxed assurance now that he was back in his safety zone. His house was nothing spectacular. It was a little brick house, two stories in a cul-de-sac. Bless could tell he felt safe. He was wrong. Fareed had taken several precautions, going around blocks, taking wrong turns purposely and other moves just to make sure he wasn't being tailed. But he was. It just wasn't a physical tail.

GPS tracked his every move.

****

"Vailsburg, huh? Goddamn, he was right under our nose the whole time," JT remarked with an ironic chuckle as he followed the GPS from Bless's phone directly to Fareed's neighborhood.Pop cocked back the pistol.

"His hot ass ain't gonna know what hit him," Pop hooted.They both broke into laughter.

****

"It's nice to meet you Bless," Fareed's wife Simone said politely.

Bless shook her hand. "You too, ma," Bless responded, thinking, *Too bad you married the wrong nigga.*

She gave Bless a subtle glance before turning away, one that he didn't miss. She was cute for a big girl, short and heavy-chested with a slight resemblance to Cora on *Meet the Browns.*

****

Outside, JT and Pop masked and gloved up.

"Fuck takin' this nigga so long?" JT fumed, but he didn't have long to wait. His phone buzzed with a text: *back door*

JT looked at Pop with a sinister grin. "Let's make it happen."

Bless had gotten his chance to make his move when he asked to use the bathroom, which was right by the back door. With one turn of the lock, he destined everybody inside to a date with the grim reaper.

JT and Pop crept through the back door quietly while Bless, Fareed, and Simone were in the living room laughing and conversing.

"Yeah fam', it's definitely good to see you," Fareed remarked."Yeah nigga, it's good to see you too."

Fareed heard the strange voice, and his blood froze in his veins. His wife opened her mouth to scream, but JT stuck the barrel of hisgun dead in it.

"Bitch, I wish you would," he hissed.

Pop smacked Fareed with his pistol, making him spit out a tooth, a glob of blood and mucus. When he recovered from the blow, Fareed looked at Bless.

"You set me up!"

Bless chuckled. "Come on, yo, don't be like that. It's just business. Give up the paper, and I give you my word you'll live."

"Money? Man, I ain't got no—"

Blah!

Pop damn near broke his jaw when he slapped him with thepistol again.

"Nigga, don't play wit' us!"

"Please, we–we don't have any money!" Simone sobbed.

Bless pulled out his gun. "Naw, bruh, don't do him like that. Dohim like this."

Boc!

Bless let off one round into the top of Fareed's knee, blowing itout until it folded in the opposite direction.

"Oooooooooooh!" Fareed bellowed like an agonizing cow. "Now . . . I'm only going to ask once. Where's the dough?"

Bless asked.

"I–I–I– swear, Bless, all the money I got is in the bedroom! Youcan have it!" Fareed cried.

"Then let's go get it," Bless demanded, grabbing him by the collar and half dragging him down the hall to the stairs.

He and JT helped him up the steps. When they got to the bedroom, Bless let Fareed's bloody and broken body slump to the floor.

"Where it at?" Bless reiterated.

"In the t-t-top drawer right there," Fareed panted, gritting through the pain.

Bless snatched the drawer and dumped its contents on the floor. It was Fareed's underwear drawer. Boxers and briefs fell out, until finally a bank envelope dropped to the floor.

A bank envelope? Bless thought as he bent to pick it up. Inside was $378. He looked at Fareed.

"Nigga, you tryin' to play me?"

"Fuck this shit, B. This nigga think it's a game," JT hollered.

He put the gun to Fareed's head and pulled the trigger.
Boc! Boc!

Fareed's brains blew out the side of his head like a piñata bursting at a child's birthday party. Shitting all over himself, he slumped, twitching to the floor.

"Yo! What the fuck you do that for? How we sposed' to find the safe?" Bless shouted, glaring at JT.

"We been here too long, yo! You shouldn't have shot him downstairs! I know somebody in this sleepy ass neighborhood heard that shit! We gotta go!" JT reasoned.

"The safe, nigga. I came for the 300 g's," Bless shouted.

"Fuck the money. Let's go!" JT spat. "The cops gonna be here any minute now."

Once Bless thought about it, he agreed. But in actuality, there never was any money, and JT knew it. He came for a homicide, not a robbery. What he told Bless was bullshit. The real deal was, Fareed had snitched on his own uncle, and his uncle wanted him dead for getting him a life sentence.

"How much we talkin'?" JT had questioned when he went tosee Fareed's uncle, Akbar.

"Ten stacks," Akbar had answered.

"Shit, for that type of money, Pop'll rape him, too!" JT joked.

Akbar chuckled, but his eyes remained serious. "I don't give a fuck what you do to him, just as long as his rat ass is dead," Akbargrowled.

"Say no more," JT assured him.

JT couldn't get close to him, but he knew Bless could. So JT used Bless, gassing him about a big lick when in actuality, Fareed was scared, broke, and in hiding.

Once they turned to the door, they heard, "Oh! Oh! Oh! Oh!"JT knew exactly what it was.

As soon as Bless and JT took Fareed upstairs, Pop stepped to Simone and put the gun to her forehead.

"Bitch, live or die?"

"L–l–l– live," she sobbed, her heavy chest heaving.

Pop pulled out his dick then said, "Then you know what to do." He grabbed her by her hair and forced her on her knees. Simone took his dick in her mouth and began working her neck, feverishly. "Yeah, you nasty bitch, eat this dick," he grunted.

The sounds of her porn performance filled the room. "Now take off your clothes."

Simone stripped so fast, it seemed like she had on a breakaway sweat suit instead of a skirt and blouse. Her breasts sagged, butthey were still firm, her nipples hard.

"Bend over," Pop instructed. She did exactly as told.

Pop spread her wide ass cheeks and slid his dick straight in her ass.

"Oh God!" she gasped, taken totally by surprise.

But Pop was surprised even more to find her ass loose and juicy, like niggas had been ass fucking her for years. "Damn this ass feel like a pussy," Pop panted, pounding Simone with all he had.

"Oh! Oh! Oh! Oh!" she moaned, hating the fact that the dick felt good to her. Before she knew it, she was throwing it back.

JT and Bless walked in.

"Yo, what the fuck?" Bless remarked, not expecting to see a live porno scene.

"That's Pop's thing. Ay yo, hurry the fuck up. We out! We leavin' yo ass right here," JT warned him.

"Hol–hol–hol up," Pop quivered, feeling a nut coming on.

As soon as he came, Simone moaned and squealed cumming right behind him. Pop pulled his dick out and pulled up his pants asSimone struggled to get on the couch.

"Naw, ma, stay right there," Pop told her. Then without hesitation, he dumped three slugs in her face.

Boc! Boc! Boc!

Half her nose got blown off, as her face exploded. Her remaining brain tissue looked like noodles.

"Now we can go." Pop chuckled.

CHAPTER NINETEEN

THE BEGINNING OF THE END

B less had been squatting in the bushes for so long his legs had fallen asleep.

"Man, where the fuck this nigga at?" Bless spat.

JT, hiding in the bush on the opposite side of the porch, replied, "Shhhh, yo. Somebody might hear you."

Pop had fallen asleep. JT elbowed him hard. "Nigga, you snorin'!"

"My bad, cuz."

Bless was fuming. His fists were balled tight and his nostrils flared. This was their third robbery since the Fareed murder, and each robbery had gotten them less than JT had promised. Once, he said the dude had several kilos of cocaine and over a hundred grand. It turned out he only had one brick and ten grand. The second time, JT said the dude had damn near half a million dollars, but he only had twenty grand and a pound of weed. Because Bless was fed up, he decided to keep everything.

JT acted as if he was vexed, but in actuality, he had

already been paid, which was why he had turned both robberies into homicides. It was the same setup as the Fareed hit. He was using Bless to hit niggas he would never have the heart to get at alone. He was gaining a name for a nigga that could knock off even the hardest-to-get niggas, but it was really Bless doing all the work.

But Bless's time was limited. He could feel the disease slowly eating him on the inside. His only solace was, the main people who had shit on him while he was locked up was dying too, and they meaning JT and Neecie who didn't even know it.

Bless was ready to do one last lick. The pharmacy. But it was bigger than just the money.

It was her. But he had to get this lick out of the way first.

The more he watched her, the more he knew he had to have her. He usually liked red bones, but there was something about her that he just couldn't get out of his head. He was drawn to her in the worse way. Even though he knew the HIV would soon be full blown AIDS, he was willing to take her with him in every way.

What is it about her? He thought.

His attraction ran deep, deeper than sex, but he didn't know it. All he knew was that she felt like what had been missing all his life and he had to have her. Even if it cost her, her life.

Bless was brought out of his thoughts when he heard the car pull up in the driveway. He clicked his nine off safety. He heard voices, but he had his back to the driveway. Yet he saw when they started up the porch stairs. Two sets of legs, a woman and a man.

"Come on, Grandma. I got you," the dude said. "Thank you, baby," she replied sweetly.

As soon as they saw the front door open, they sprang intoaction.

"Don't fuckin' move, nigga!" JT barked as he put the gun to theback of dude's head and forced him inside.

"Oh Lord Jesus!" Grandma exclaimed as Bless pushed herinside too.

Pop was the last one in and slammed the door behind them.

JT made dude get face down while he frisked him for a weapon.

He found a revolver in his waist.

"Oh, you was gonna shoot me, nigga? Huh?" JT barked, then slapped the dude several times with his own pistol, causing him to hit the floor.

"Yo, chill B. Chill. You got it! Tell Mook I'ma get his money!"

JT kicked him in the mouth to shut him up. "Who? Nigga, youowe me! Now where is it?"

"In the bedroom yo! It's all I got!"

JT snatched him off the floor and pushed him toward the back. "Yo, I got Grandma!" Pop exclaimed.

Bless frowned up. "Nigga, you can't be serious!" Pop shrugged. "Grandma need love, too!"

Bless shook his head as he walked out of the room. By the time he turned the corner into the back, he heard the gunshots.

Boc! Boc!

When he walked in, the dude had a big hole in his chest that left a puddle of blood across the carpet. JT stood over an open safewith stacks of money inside.

"Jackpot, nigga!" JT cackled.

"That don't look like no two hundred thousand yo," Bless grumbled.

"It's at least fifty," JT countered, adding, "Shit, it's better than last time."

"Yeah, and I'm takin' fuckin' half."

Before JT could respond, they heard, "Oh Lord! Lord! Please stop!"

JT chuckled, but Bless wasn't amused. "Ay yo, your cousin sick as fuck."

They bagged up the money in a trash bag, then headed out the door. When they walked in the living room, they saw a familiar butwicked sight. Pop had grandma's old ass bent over the couch.

"Please, get him off me!" she screamed. "No doubt, Grandma," JT replied.

Boc! Boc!

He sent two to her head.

Her head jerked back spewing brain all over Pop's bare stomach. "Yo!" Pop jumped back, dick quivering.

"You wanted brains, right? Bring yo' nasty ass on!" JT spat. "Yo, Pop! We lucky if there's fifty grand in here. What the fuck

kinda shit is y'all on?" Bless spat, unable to hold back. "Nigga, that's fifteen grand apiece," guilty JT interjected.

"I'm not talking to you." Bless cut across the room and stood in JT's face.

Y'all keep wasting my time with this little shit. Y'all small-mindedmuthafuckas! Bless shoved JT.

"Yo, yo, yo! Cut the bullshit. We can handle this at the

spot." Pop got in between them.

"We better handle this somewhere. Because I'm walking away with more than fifteen grand," Bless threatened as he left thehouse.

****

When Bless got back to Neecie's apartment, she was already asleep, wearing nothing but a pajama top. She lay curled up on her side, and in the moonlight, looked like the sweetest and finest woman in the world. But by the light of reality, the only thing sweet about her was her pussy. She was a straight-up hood rat.Born and bred and would probably die without ever knowing any other way to be. He thought how crazy the hood was to spawn motherfuckers like himself, JT, Pop, and Neecie, each with their own kind of crazy. A part of him felt sorry for her, but that part was small, weak, and getting weaker by the day. Bottom line, she, along with JT had left him for dead when he went to prison, disrespected him and now he would leave them both to die a slow death. *Who gets the last laugh now?*

Bless undressed at the foot of the bed, and by the time he was naked, he was already rock hard—her top was too short to cover her pretty brown ass. Her cheeks were looking juicy, like they would squirt if he squeezed them.

He lifted her top leg and slid his dick up in her from the side, surprised to find that her pussy was wet, even while she wasasleep.

"Ooooooooh, Bless," she cooed, coming out of her sleep. "I love when you wake me up like thisssss."

Bless sucked on her neck as he long-dicked her nice and

slow. "Damn, I missed this pussy while I was gone," he grunted.

"Did you, baby? We missed you too. Oh, Bless, wait– ohhhh fuck—that's my spot!"

He pushed himself deep inside her, grinding on her spot whilehe patted her clit. Neecie thought she would lose her mind.

"Da-daddy, oh, God, you're the best!" Neecie squealed, her body bucking as she squirted hard.

Bless pulled her up on her knees, forcing her face into thepillow by gripping her by the back of her neck. He watched his dick go in and out, her pussy extra creamy. He could see it at the base of his dick in the moonlight. The bed springs sang a song of mercy while Neecie sang lead.

"Fuck me, daddy, fuck me real good! Oh . . . ohhh . . . right here, shit!" Neecie panted, throwing it back and taking his back shots like a pro.

Bless slid his thumb in her ass as he pounded her furiously. He knew this would be the last time he fucked her, so he wanted to make sure he gave it all to her, literally.

"Turn around and swallow this nut," he demanded.

"Yes, daddy," she said, flipping over on her ass, then taking Bless's dick in her mouth.

Her pussy started cumming again because she loved the feel ofa big dick down her throat. Bless was in a zone. Between the tight, slickness of her throat and the eye contact she gave him while she did it, he didn't last long, cumming down her throat, then wiping the rest on her lips. Exhausted, he lay down beside her.

Neecie wiped the sweat from his forehead, gazing down

at him with a smile of satisfaction on her face and asked, "You hate me, don't you?"

The question took him by surprise, so at first he couldn't answer. Then he finally replied, "Naw ma, I don't hate you. But it is fucked up how you left me for dead, and then had babies by a nigga that's supposed to be my man. But fuck it. That's how the game go, right?"

Neecie shook her head. "It wasn't like that, Bless. I do love you, but you left me. What was I supposed to do? And as for JT, thatshit is drug-related. I mean, we were at the club poppin' mollies, and I was horny as fuck. One thing led to another," she explained.

"Two times? Neecie, you got two kids by the nigga."

"I used him to fill the void you left, Bless. Shit, it's just like you said. I already had one baby by him. And it felt like me and you—we'd never be the same, you know, never like together- together. So I ain't think you would trip," she answered.

"I'm not," he lied, refusing to wear his emotions on his sleeve. Neecie leaned down and kissed him on the forehead. "Baby,

I'm sorry if I hurt you. No matter what happens, I'll always be here for you," she vowed, then lay down and cuddled up beside him.

Bless felt a twinge of regret. Soon, she wouldn't be there for anyone because he had given her and JT a death sentence with a quiet count.

****

At 5:00 a.m. Bless's eyes popped open. After being in prison somany years, his body could tell time on its own.

Today was the day. To everyone else it was Valentine's Day. But to him it was payday. He got up and took a shower, the whole while seeing Ebony's face. An obsession. He had to have her.

Once he was dressed, he looked down at Neecie sleeping serenely again. He went in his bag because he had something for her. It was a home AIDS test. On top was a big red bow and a card that read Happy Valentine's Day.

"The gift that keeps on giving." He chuckled, and then he walked out forever.

CHAPTER TWENTY

BACK TO EBONY . . .

Ebony sat on her balcony smoking a joint and watching the heavy rain fall down. Flashes of lightning provided the only light because the storm had knocked the power out on her block. As she watched the raindrops drench the street, the wind whipping and whirling, sending debris everywhere, she could feel a similar storm within.

The doctor had been right. All these years, it hadn't been about making the guilty suffer, it had been about her suffering, her pain, her need to be loved and needed. Deep down she had known it for a long time, but she hid it from herself, making herself feel like the victim when she was really the predator, the hunter . . . And that's exactly what it was. A hunt. The storm brought back the memory of the first time she had gone after someone other than a molester, when she first realized she was out of control . . .

The bar had been a neighborhood spot. The kind found on every other corner in the hood. A place where the lonely never drank alone, and people laughed loud to keep from crying hard. Ebony sat at the bar. She was on her third drink, but she was acting drunker than she really was. Three goons noticed her.

"Yo, check that shorty at the bar," the skinny goon said, elbowing the chunky goon.

"Which one? The Puerto Rican bitch?"

"Naw, the dark skinned one wit' the short hair."

The short goon guffawed. "Man, that ugly ass bitch? You sure it ain't a man?"

The chunky goon laughed and downed his drink. Skinny got offended because he felt like his boy was trying to play him.

"Nigga, fuck you, that ain't no goddamn man. She got some pretty ass lips," he remarked, gripping his crotch just imagining what she could do with them.

"Shit, I can't front, she is kinda sexy," Chunky admitted. "Nigga, you just drunk!" Short laughed.

Skinny stood up, adjusting his crotch. "Where you goin?" Chunky questioned.

"Where you think? That's easy pussy. She ugly and she drunk!" Ebony heard every word. Being called ugly had stopped bothering her a long time ago. Now, it was so much a part of her, she accepted it as reality.

She felt Skinny approach and met him with a smile. He knew he was fucking.

"What's good, ma? What you drinkin'?"

"Shit, whateva you buyin'," Ebony replied, voice slurred.

Skinny's dick got hard just off anticipation. "Yo Benny! Lemme get two grey gooses!"

A few minutes later, the bartender brought over the drinks. Bythen, Skinny was already knee deep in his game.

"So what's your name?" he questioned.

Ebony sipped her drink then looked him in his eyes and bluntlyreplied, "Does it matter?"

Skinny smirked. "Naw, it don't. So what you tryin' to get into?"Ebony shrugged. "What did you have in mind?"

"Well, you know what I'm sayin', I'm just tryin' to chill, feel me?" Skinny stammered, because he wasn't used to a womanbeing so straight forward.

Ebony snickered. "Why don't you speak your mind? I like a nigga that's about his."

Feeling like his manhood was being challenged, he spat back, "Shit, I'm tryin' to fuck."

Ebony downed her drink, licked her lips seductively, then answered, "I thought you'd never ask." She tried to get off the stool, but faked like she stumbled.

Skinny caught her. "Whoa, lil mama! You good?"

"I'm grrrrreat!" she slurred like Tony the Tiger. Then shelaughed.

When they got outside, she noticed Chunky and Short had come out right behind them.

"Who are they?"

"Oh naw, that's my mans and 'em. They just gonna drop usoff," Skinny said, winking at Short on the low.

Ebony shrugged and said, "Whateva."

Watching the sway in her low slung hips in her tight little skirt, Chunky couldn't help but curse under his breath, "Damn, lil'mama workin' it!"

Short was driving. Chunky sat in the front passenger seat, with Skinny and Ebony in the back.

"Just wake me when we get to your spot," Ebony said, lying her head on Skinny's shoulder and acting like she was asleep.

Short glanced in the rearview. "Damn, that bitch drunk as fuck."

Chunky looked over the seat, the lust beginning to color his eyes. "And she got some thick ass thighs. Ay yo, my nigga, push up that skirt, let a nigga see that padow!"

Skinny wiggled his shoulder to see if she was sleep. She appeared to be out cold. He laid her back on the seat and hiked her skirt up until he found she wasn't wearing any panties.

"Goddamn! This bitch ain't got on no panties!" Skinny exclaimed.

"Her pussy fatta than a muhfucka!" Chunky chimed in.

Short damn near crashed trying to look over his seat and drive at the same time.

"Man, fuck that! I'm fuckin' this bitch now!" Skinny spat, unbuckling his pants. He cocked one of her legs up on the seat and one over his shoulder. Her cleanly shaved pink pussy sat up like a monkey's fist just waiting to take a dick.

Ebony groaned as if she were just coming to. "Wh–what are you doin'?" she slurred, her voice hoarse and small.

"I'm tryin' to see what this pussy about," Skinny replied, taking his pants down to his knees, his hard dick throbbing in his hand.

"Don–don't do this," she protested weakly. She called that her warning, her attempt to justify to herself that they were doing it to themselves and not the other way around.

150

But if her words had been a red light, Skinny ran straight through it.

He grabbed her other leg by the ankle and rested it on his shoulder, then he slid his dick into her sho' nuff pussy trap.

"Ssssss, ooohhh dammnnnn," she cooed like she was sliding slowly into a zone. Skinny started long-dicking her and loving the way she was meeting his every thrust.

"Yo nigga, pull this muhfucka over!" Chunky barked, ready to get his.

"Wait, baby. Hit this pussy from the back," Ebony begged,pushing Skinny up.

By then Short had parked deep in a darkened apartment building parking lot. Ebony turned and bent over. Skinny spread her pussy cheeks and pushed his dick deep inside.

Chunky snatched opened the door. The fuck faces she was making had him hard as a rock.

"Yes, yes, yesssss," Ebony sang, but her eyes should've been their hell no!

Chunky took out his fat sausage and filled her mouth with it.

She slurped it up like a pro.

"Yo nigga, hurry up!" Short gruffed at Skinny, already taking his hard dick out just watching Ebony work from both ends.

"Hol' up, shit! Goddamn!" Skinny cursed because the pussy had him in a zone. He burst deep inside her, until his cum ran out of her pretty pink pussy and down her thigh.

One down, two to go, Ebony thought.

Short couldn't wait until Skinny backed up. He pulled

straight up to her bumper and gave her all seven and half inches.

"Damn this ugly bitch can fuck!" Short grunted, bouncing her up and down with his punishing back hits.

Short pulled his dick out just in time to bust all over Ebony's lips, nose, and chin. She ran her tongue over her lips and licked it off.

"Mmmmm, taste like caramel." Ebony giggled.

"Yo, sit her on your dick. Let me get at this asshole," Skinny lusted, his dick already ready for round two.

"Man, I ain't into that porno shit," Short responded.
"Man, fuck that! I am!" Chunky exclaimed.

Chunky lay on the backseat and Ebony straddled him. Skinny got behind her and slid his dick in her ass while Chunky fucked her pussy. She had never been fucked like that before, so the combination had her cumming all over the place.

"I–I can't stop cumminnnnn!" she squealed, her pussy squirting for the first time.

Short was mesmerized by the sight. He couldn't resist jumping in.

"Nigga, I thought you wasn't wit' this porno shit?" Chunky teased.

"Man, fuck that, this off tha hook!"

He slid his dick in Ebony's mouth, completing the freak show.

Seven months later, Skinny and Short found out they were HIV positive.

Ebony had done her job well.

The rain tapping on the balcony window snapped Ebony from the past. She left the balcony and went inside. From the outside, the streaks looked like they were on the window, but they were also on Ebony's cheeks. She knew that night she had crossed the line. It was also the first time she tried to kill herself.

THE BEGINNING

CHAPTER TWENTY-ONE

BACK TO BLESS . . .

"Ma, why I gotta go to the doctor all the time?" a six-year- old Bless asked his mother as they walked into the lobby of the doctor's building.

Mrs. Wiggins pressed the button for the elevator, then looked down at him with an angelic, motherly smile. "Boy, stop complaining. You only have to go twice a year."

"It seems like all the time," he pouted, adding, "And I ain't sick."

"Let's hope so," she said under her breath, in a voice only meant for God's ears.

When the elevator swooshed open, Bless folded his arms across his little chest. "I'm not going! I'm not sick! I hate that thing they stick in my mouth!" he continued to pout.

Mrs. Wiggins sighed. "Boy, don't tell me what you ain't gonna do. Now come on here before I call your father," she threatened.

One mention of his father, and he slowly but surely

dragged his feet and got on the elevator. As it ascended, she could tell his reluctance wasn't rebellion, it was fear. The same fear she felt for him every time he had to make this trip.

"Baby, listen. I know you're scared. And it's okay to be scared. Even big boys get scared. But don't worry, I'll be there with you, okay?" she assured him and took his hand.

"Okay, Mommy," he agreed. "I love you, my blessing."

"I love you too, Mommy."

It was the same routine every six months. The tenseness. The doctor's visit. The wait. Temporary relief. Repeat. For four years the routine had never changed. Until then.

One week later. . .

"Lord Jesus, Lord, my God, I–I–I–I don't know what you want me to do! Please give me the strength to give my baby strength, Lord! Ain't this child been through enough? I'm not questioning you, Lord, but he got so much against him already. How he gonna bear up under this?" Mrs. Wiggins cried, tears drenching her face.

Even Mr. Wiggins, a man who didn't pray much and never cried, was on his knees beside her, doing both. When his wife couldn't go on, he just hugged her to him and held her with all the love in his heart.

Several minutes later, when they both had gotten themselves together enough to rise up off their knees and go to Bless's room, Mr. Wiggins took her hand as they made their way to him.

They knocked then entered. He was sitting on his bed Indian style, holding a basketball and watching the Knicks game.

"Baby . . ." Mrs. Wiggins began, fighting back the tears as she approached.

Mr. Wiggins had to take over. "Son, turn off the TV. We needto talk to you," he instructed him gently.

Bless hit the remote's off button, turned to his parents, and said,"I have AIDS, don't I?"

"Oh, Lord Jesus!" Mrs. Wiggins sobbed, sitting on the edge of the bed.

"Don't cry, Mama. I figured I did. I can feel it inside me," Bless remarked calmly, reaching over and taking his mother's hand.

"You're a very brave young man, you know that? Do you know how much we love you and how glad we are that you're a part of our lives?" his father asked him.

Bless nodded. "I know and I'm gonna be okay. Don't worry about me. God will protect me," Bless responded confidently.

Mrs. Wiggins hugged him. "You give me such strength." She beamed.

And over the coming years, she realized that dealing with a special needs child may be a labor of love, but it was truly a labor. Every day she administered various meds, from a steroid, an immune booster, and AZT, all in liquid form because of his young age.

But it began to take a toll on their lives, their livelihood, and their marriage. Mrs. Wiggins began to drink to kill the pain of knowing her Blessing was slowly becoming her curse. Mr. Wiggins soon lost his job, which only added to the stress.

One night, when Bless was twelve, he woke up in the

middle of the night to go to the bathroom, he heard them arguing.

"Bills, bill, bills! That's all I hear out yo' goddamn mouth!" Mr. Wiggins barked. "Don't you think I'm trying to get a job? What are you doing all day besides drinkin' yourself to death?"

"I take care of our son!" she shot back, the vodka in her veins making her sway slightly in her stance.

Mr. Wiggins laughed. "Our son? He's not our son, or have you forgotten?" Mr. Wiggins snapped.

"Lower your voice, David! He may hear you!"

Bless did hear him, and it made him flinch. Not because he didn't know he was adopted, that was something they never hid from him. It made him flinch because he had never heard his father speak in such a cruel way. The words brought tears to his eyes quicker than any wisecrack ever could.

"This is not about him, it's about us! We can't afford this! When he was just a foster child and the state was paying for everything, it wasn't a problem. But now that I lost my job and he's our adopted son, we can't keep up with the medical expenses! I love Jermaine just as much as you do, but—"

"No! You can't love him talking like that, David! He is my son! Maybe not biologically, but he is my blessing from God. God will make a way!" Mrs. Wiggins declared.

Mr. Wiggins sighed and shook his head. "But I'm being practical, Leslie."

Bless could hear his mother sobbing, but it was no less than his own. He went back to his room, forgetting all about his bladder. He knew his parents loved him, but like his father had said, he was just being practical. And hadn't his father always told him, a man stands on his own two feet? He looked at himself in the mirror and watched the only tears he would ever cry, dry up in his eyes.

"From now on I'ma be my own man," he vowed to his reflection.

He grabbed the forty-two dollars he had saved, whatever clothes he could fit in his book bag, and a twelve-year-old Bless went out his window, never looking back.

******

It didn't take long before Bless's money ran out. His clothes were sticking to his body and his ribs were beginning to touch. He had a natural sense of survival, which made him resourceful and saved him from freezing to death. But eating was another matter entirely. The soup kitchen lines didn't pay off all the time.

"Sorry kid, we don't have anything else to give out," the kind college student told him, after he had waited in line an hour, only to be the next person to be served right when the food ran out.

Just hearing the words made his stomach growl with loud protest. "Man, please. I ain't ate all day," he pleaded, his hunger stronger than his pride.

"Look," the college student said, gesturing to the empty pots.

The look of dejection on Bless's young face made the college student relent. He sighed, went into his pocket, and handed Bless a five dollar bill. "Make it last," he advised.

"Thank you," Bless replied sincerely. Even the smallest gesture of human kindness could touch a desperate soul. Bless turned to walk away.

"Ay kid."

Bless turned around.

"I don't know if you know, but restaurants dump their food about fifteen minutes before closing. Get there before anyone else does," he explained.

"Good look," Bless answered, jogging off.

The college student watched the young boy jog off and mumbled, "Yeah kid, good luck. You're gonna need it."

For a couple of nights, Bless was in heaven. He found a few restaurants that dumped their food at the same time every evening. At first, eating out of a dumpster disgusted him. But hunger made him get over that real quick . . .

Until he went to Dunkin' Donuts.

He had never been to Dunkin' Donuts at closing, but when the lady bought out the trays of donuts, bagels, and sandwiches and threw them inside the dumpster, he was all over them in an instant.

"Ay!"

Bless was so into his donuts he hadn't even noticed the big, bulky figure of a man who had climbed into the dumpster behind him.

"Ay nigga, what the fuck you doin' in my dumpster?" the beefy bum growled.

Bless dropped the half eaten donut. "I–I was hungry," Bless uttered.

"Nigga, I don't give a fuck if you were starvin'! Get the fuck outta my shit!"

Bless tried to grab two handfuls before jumping out, but he lost his footing on a soft spot in the trash and fell face-first in a puddle of cooking grease. He tried to get up, but the bum grabbed him by the collar with one hand, then punched him as if he was a grown man with the other.

"Nigga, drop my shit! I'ma teach you about stealin' people's shit!"

Bless tried to punch back, and although his fists were landing, they were having no effect on the vagrant. But the bum's blows were definitely having an effect on him. Every blow seemed like it was breaking something, and when it was all said and done, Bless's jaw and two of his ribs were broken.

"If. I. Ever. Catch. You. Here. Again. I'ma. Kill. You!" the bum raged, punching him to the rhythm of every word.

Bless knew the bum was trying to kill him. He could feel himself slipping into darkness, a darkness he feared would be permanent. He stuck his hand down into the trash, searching desperately for something to defend himself with.

His desperate fingers met with some cold metal. The handle was broken, but the blade wasn't. Bless gripped it, and with all the energy he had left, he came up with the knife and stabbed the transient dead in his eye socket.

"Aaaaaggghhh!" he screamed, trying to get away from Bless just as fast as he jumped on him.

Bless now had the upper hand, and he damn sure wasn't about to give up his advantage. Fear made him puncture the bum's eye, but it was rage, pent up, uncontrollable rage that made him forget his pain, stab him in the face, the neck, the throat, the chest, over and over and over until the bum's face looked like a pepperoni pizza. Blood spurted everywhere, and the bum was no longer moving.

Bless, chest heaving, finally stopped. When he looked

down at the dead bum's face, he felt no remorse. He only wished he could do it again because of the pain he had caused him. Once more he stabbed the knife into the bum's chest and left it there. He grabbed a handful of donuts and yanked the knife, his new weapon of protection, out of the bum, and struggled out of the dumpster.

The bum had been hollering and screaming at the top of his lungs, alerting the store manager inside. He came out to see what was going on, peeped in the dumpster, and saw Bless stabbing the bum as if he was starring in a Chucky movie. He ran inside and yelled, "There's a kid in the dumpster stabbing somebody up!"

Bless couldn't have picked a worse place to catch his first body, because cops love donuts more than killing niggas. One of the four officers drew his weapon and ran out, followed by the other three.

As soon as he got outside, he saw Bless half falling, half jumping out of the dumpster, an armful of donuts and a bloody knife still in his right hand.

"Freeze! Drop the weapon!" he screamed, dropping to one knee, his gun trained on Bless's head.

Bless didn't hesitate to do just that. "Now! Put your hands up in the air!" "I-I can't! My ribs!" Bless cried out. "Get down now!"

"I can't!"

Boc! Boc! Boc!

Two shots hit Bless high in the chest, but his body was so frail they went right through. The searing pain made him wish for death as he dropped the knife and stumbled forward, falling onto his face and blacking out.

******

"Son . . . can you hear me? Look at me. Do you know what happened to you?" the doctor asked.

Bless was just regaining consciousness two days later. The first thing he saw was the white haired, black doctor with the grandfatherly smile.

"I . . . I got shot. They killed me," Bless replied.

"And what about before that?" asked the pock-faced detective standing behind the doctor.

The detective stepped up to his bedside.

"Detective, this young man is too weak for an interrogation," the doctor protested.

"Thanks, Doc, but I'll take it from here. He may be your patient, but he's my suspect," the detective smugly responded.

The doctor, having been raised to be subservient to white men, relented and walked out, leaving Bless under the hostile care of thedetective.

"Okay, kid, answer the question. Why did you kill that guy?"Bless glared at him.

The detective smirked. "Oh, we've got a tough guy, huh? I love tough guys. They always scream the loudest."

Bless went to move his arm but found it was cuffed. It surprisedhim, and the detective read the look.

"Get used to it, tough guy. I've seen your work. You're a cold- blooded killer. Good thing we caught you early, because now I'm gonna bury you!" the detective seethed.

Bless looked him in the eyes and replied, "I'm already dead."He turned his head and closed his eyes.

The detective didn't know how to respond, until a

few days later when he found out Bless was HIV positive. But it didn't make a difference. The detective wanted to make sure Bless went to prison. After seeing the way Bless savagely butchered the bum in the dumpster, the detective wouldn't rest until Bless was safely behind bars. He even wanted to charge him as an adult with first degree murder.

"Look, I know killers, okay? And I know some of you bleeding heart liberals would love to save this kid from himself. But take it from me—he's a headline waiting to happen. This kid had death written all over him!" the detective ranted to the district attorney.

******

"Listen, the D.A.'s offering you a plea for second degree. I suggest you take it, Bless," his no-good public defender suggested between bites of a ham and cheese on rye. They were in the visiting room at the juvenile detention center.

"But he tried to kill me!" Bless emphasized.

The public defender shrugged, licked the mustard from his thumb and replied, "Your word against thirty-seven stab wounds. Self-defense is one thing, but you took it overboard."

Bless may've been young, but he knew he was done. Hell, he belonged to the state. The only alternative was going to trial with a lawyer who wouldn't hesitate to sell him out.

"I want—"

"Kid, your foster parents aren't' coming to get you. You know you belong to the state. The state is your parents. So let's get this over with."

"Yeah yo . . . I'll take the plea."

He was sentenced to be held until he was eighteen years old, which was basically what they called juvenile life. As soon as he arrived, he knew he was going to have problems.

"John Doe?" the CO read, holding Bless's commitment papers. He looked at Bless. "You can't be serious. Who the fuck do you think you are?"

Bless, standing naked (because the first thing you do when you come to prison is strip), simply shrugged. "Ask the fuckin' court."

His arrest records read John Doe because he refused to give his name. He didn't want the Wiggins to see what he had become.

The CO stepped in his face. "Cuss me one more goddamn time, and I promise you I'll snatch the voice box out of your throat," he gritted in Bless's face.

"Man, fuck you!" Bless barked.

Blah!

"Code two! Code two!" went out the call over the radio.

The officer knocked Bless down with his baton, and then the other three officers joined in. The other four naked juveniles stepped out of the way as the officers beat and stomped Bless's naked body, then dragged him half-conscious to the hole. They didn't bring him a stitch of clothes or a mat for three days. The cell, a small four by six sized cubicle, smaller than an apartment bathroom only had a toilet. They kept it cold in the room. Bless didpushups to stay warm and until he was exhausted. On the third day,the sergeant came to his door.

"You ready to behave yourself?"

Bless howled like a wolf in the sergeant's face, then laughedlike a mad man.

"Fucking crazy asshole!" the sergeant spat, then walked away.

He used everything that life was throwing at him to fuel his anger. It was only the anger that kept him warm three more days, until they saw they couldn't break him and finally let him out and put him into population.

Word had already spread about the new dude who cursed the meanest officer in the facility to his face. Of course, the story got exaggerated.

"Man, I heard dude told Ramsey to go fuck his mother!"

"I heard he spit in Ramsey's face!"

"Naw, he told Ramsey to go fuck his mother, spit in his face, then slapped Ramsey like a bitch! If it wasn't for the other officers,the kid would've beat him to death!"

Bless hadn't been in prison a hot week and was already a yard legend. So by the time he stepped in the pod, niggas were ready to be on his team. Except one.

Storm.

He may've been only sixteen, but he was truly a storm. At five foot nine inches and wiry, he had been a Golden Glove champ twice by the time he was thirteen, the year he got locked up for killing a whole family for a drug debt. They charged him as an adult, and he was given a natural life sentence, meaning he was never going home. Meaning, he looked at prison as his home, and he damn sure wasn't about to let a nigga it.

Storm watched Bless come in with his mat and lay it on the top bunk over a kid named JT.

"What up, fam? I done heard all about you. They call me JT," he introduced himself. Bless sized up the little brown-skinned dude who reminded him of Nas, chipped tooth and all. He would come to find out JT was a shark and from Newark, which made them a team, but at the moment, he just looked like a cool nigga.

"What up? I'm Bless."

"Bless? What you, a Five Percenter? A God body?" "Naw," Bless replied as he unpacked.

JT shrugged and let it go.

"So, I heard you slapped the shit outta Ramsey.""Who?"

"Officer Ramsey in receiving," JT explained.

Even though he was new to prison, he knew the value of reputation, even if it was a little inflated.

"Oh. I don't know his name," Bless replied nonchalantly.

JT looked around, sizing up the situation. He saw Storm with his crew over by the TV area, watching Bless. He didn't really like Storm, but he wasn't big enough to go against him. He didn't know if Bless was up for it, but instinct told him to bet his chips on Bless.

"Ay, look yo, I know we just met but check it. That freckled- faced nigga over by the TV, the one that thinks he Floyd Mayweather, that's Storm. The nigga think he run the dorm. I know he gonna try you. If you want, I could get you a banger," JT offered.

Bless looked at him. "Why? They gonna try and jump me?""Naw. That nigga just nice wit' his hands."

Bless smirked. "So am I."

It wasn't long before they found out who was nicer. Once the CO made their rounds and left the pod, Storm, followed by his crew, approached Bless.

"Ay yo, my man, what size is them Nikes?" Storm challenged.Bless grabbed his crotch. "Your size, nigga!"

The pod got quiet, and all eyes turned to see what the new kidon the block was about.

"Word?" Storm smirked. "How 'bout you come holla at me in the shower."

"Nigga, you pussy? You need a team for one man?" Bless spat.Storm smirked. "Naw yo, it's a fair one."

"Say no more."

Bless and Storm stepped in the shower. The other dudes and JT formed a circle around them. As soon as they did, Storm and Bless locked hands. Storm had such a quick jab, he had already tagged Bless three times before Bless got in one blow. Bless was no matchfor Storm's boxing skills, but Storm couldn't fuck with Bless's street-fighting style, where anything goes, including picking a nigga up and slamming him on his back, knocking the wind out of him.

"Oomph!" Storm gasped as his head hit the wet tile. Once Bless got on top of him, he began to punish Storm.

"Naw, fuck that!" one of Storm's partners barked, then hooked Bless in the ear.

From there it was on. JT hit the nigga that hit Bless, then another dude hit JT. After that, the rest of Storm's crew jumped Bless and JT, but at the bottom of the pile, Bless and Storm were going blow for blow.

For the next six years, Bless and JT were tight. The only thing JT didn't know was that Bless had HIV. He knew he took medication, but he didn't know the specifics of his illness. They both were released when they turned eighteen. Both went back to Newark, New Jersey, got with

Pop and wreaked havoc together. Bless was the one who gained the most respect because of his level head. Bless was the bravest and made sure he kept their pockets fat. With that, came the chicks, including Neecie, the fine red-bone.

JT was a liar and nine times out of ten his word was not bond. He often played the background and wasn't taken seriously. But Bless always had his back. So much so that when they got busted with a package, Bless took the weight and did the two years. That made Bless even more credible and kept his name alive on the streets while JT still had to play the shadows

It wasn't until Bless's second bid, when he got sent up Upstate, that he now had full blown AIDS and began slacking up on taking his meds. He was just tired.

"You muhfuckas can't make me live!" Bless barked from his isolation cell. He only had two weeks left when he decided he was tired of taking medications. All his life he had to take meds just to live, but he had run out of reasons to want to be alive.

Until he saw her.

CHAPTER TWENTY-TWO

BACK TO EBONY

Ebony was back in Dr. Jenson's office. She had made up her mind that this would be her last time. She figured that she had gotten all there was out of the sessions.

This time she didn't want to sit in front of him. She wanted to try the couch, figuring it might be fun.

"Doc, do you mind if I lay on the couch like they do in the movies?"

Dr. Jenson peered over his wire frames. "If that will make you more comfortable, sure. I have no problem with that. He stood and picked up his notepad from off his desk. Ebony had already slipped off her shoes and was getting comfortable.

"This makes me feel important. Is this normal, Doc?"

"Feeling important or wanting to lie on the couch?" He chuckled.

"Both."

"Perfectly," he told her.

She couldn't help but giggle as she pressed her body into the velvety material. "Okay, Doc, fire away."

Dr. Jenson smiled. "Fire away? I only have one question today, which I think would help me a lot with your case. I need you to tellme something. There had to be someone in your life who showed you love and affection. Did you have at least one relationship? Who was he? Tell me about him." Dr. Jenson watched her for a reaction.

Ebony turned away from him and curled up in a ball. Her jovial spirit no longer caressed the room. She began to cry.

Her first thoughts went to the love she had for her long lost brother. Then she began to think back to the only man she knew who had truly loved her.

She had just gotten out of the hospital after her first suicide attempt. It was a bittersweet return to the world. How disappointed she had been to open her eyes and see that she was still alive. It feltworse than waking up roasting in hell. But after a few weeks of counseling, she realized how beautiful life could be. Yet, stepping out, back on her own, left to her own loneliness. Ebony felt like Billie Holliday singing "Good Morning Heartache." On top of that, when she returned to her apartment, she found an eviction notice. And later she discovered she had lost her job, which was to be expected, but she knew it would be hell starting over from scratch. So she wasn't in the best of moods as she was crossing the street, only to be bumped and jostled by oncoming foot traffic. She felt like an exhausted swimmer being rolled over by the under current. Ebony elbowed her way through the crowd, only to be bumped so hard by a man rounding the corner, she dropped her phone and the screen cracked.

"Goddamn, why don't you watch where you're going?" she spazzed. She was ready to throw hands, win, lose, or draw.

"I can't," he replied with an ironic grin on his face.

It was then that she noticed the dark glasses. He was blind. Her anger abated slightly.

"Well, maybe you should wear a sign."

He laughed and the brightness in its tone made her smile too. "That was a good one. Maybe I will."

He may've been blind, but Ebony wasn't, and she could damn sure see he was cute. Smooth caramel skin and juicy, suckable lips.His looks helped relieve the tension.

"I'm sorry. I'm just having a bad day," Ebony admitted.

"I think we've all had one of those from time to time. If you want, we can go pushing down blind guys. I'll be your getaway driver," he joked.

She laughed harder than she had in years. She laughed so hard, she cried, and then she cried for real because she was a mixed bag of emotions and didn't know how to be happy.

"Again I'm sorry, but I have to go," she said, then tried to rush off.

He gently took her by the wrist, something she had seen Jamie Foxx do in the movie *Ray*, so she thought she knew what he was doing.

"What's wrong? Why are you crying?"

She was surprised he could sense the tears she had gotten so adept at hiding. "I—I'm— it's just been rough and—" she stammered, trying to cram a whole fucked up lifetime into one sentence.

He cut her off gently. "Listen, why don't we go have a bite to eat, okay? I'm hungry for your company," he said with a subtle smirk.

Ebony couldn't say no.

He took her to a Citte Bistro around the corner that boasted umbrella'ed sidewalk tables and Paninis so light and buttery they almost floated off the plate.

"Anything else, Terrence?" the Latina-looking waitress asked with a pleasant smile.

Ebony felt a ping of jealousy that this gorgeous woman knewhis name and could be so familiar.

"Ebony, you need anything else?" he asked.

"No thank you," she answered, grateful for his consideration. He turned his face in the waitress's direction. "We're good,

Natalie."

"Let me know," she replied, then she walked away.

Terrence sipped his expresso. "Now, we've been talking for over an hour, and you've told me everything but what's wrong. I may be blind but I can see." He chuckled.

Ebony shook her head. She didn't know how to take the situation. She was having lunch with a fine, considerate, and charming man, but all she could think about was whether he would've even given her the time of day if he could see. Ebony imagined him having bumped into her, not even looking at her, but looking through her and dismissing her from his conscious. The thought made her mad, and she could feel the bitterness she kept bottled up inside, beginning to bubble.

"Terrence, can I ask you something?""Yes."

"Why do you even care?"

He took a deep breath and let out a sympathetic sigh. "Because. I see with my ears and with my hands. What I feel paints the picture of my world. And what I saw the moment you bumped into me felt like a cold spring, tightly wound and ready to explode. What I felt was the beginning of an earthquake inside of you, and when you spoke . . ." he shook his head, "No one should have that much pain inside. That's why I care. Because I know it's there."

By the time he was finished, Ebony's body was wracked with sobs. No one, not even the counselors at the hospital, had read her so deeply and completely. Nothing in the world felt as good as being understood, and in that moment she felt relief.

Terrence stood and felt his way to the seat next to Ebony and put his arm around her. She clung to him like a child to its mother and cried into his chest. She didn't care that people walking by witnessed her break down. In fact, it made her feel good for the world to see her being loved.

When she got herself together, she wiped her eyes and sat up. "I'm so sorry. You probably think I'm crazy."

Terrence handed her a napkin. "Not at all, Ebony. Life hits us when we least expect it. I'm just glad that I could be a part of yours."

The sincerity in his voice touched her to her core, so much so, she felt the need to tell him, "I . . . I am HIV positive."

She watched his face, waiting for him to cringe, frown, or simply get up and walk away. But to her surprise, he did none of those things. Instead, he took her hand and said, "And now you also have a friend."

They walked to the park, talking along the way. Finally

feeling unburdened, she told him everything. About her suicide attempts, Miss Cat, the loss of her family, and how she had lost her job and her apartment after she got out of the hospital.

"So basically, I'm homeless and unemployed. I-I don't know what I'm going to do," she admitted.

He nodded and turned his face in the direction of the sun. "The sun is setting, isn't it?"

"Yes, how did you know?"

Terrence smiled knowingly. "I can feel it. But it will rise again.

It always does, you know?"

She nodded, but then remembered he couldn't see. "Yes. It does."

"Come on. Let's go home," he said, holding out his hand with the sincerest smile she'd ever seen to go along with it. She knew what he was offering, and she took it without hesitation.

The next two months were like heaven for Ebony. She had never been in such a loving environment. Terrence was a sculptor by day and a trumpet player in a small quartet at night. She had never been around so much creativity in her life, and it made her feel creative as well. Ebony started writing small poems, poems she never shared, but they made her feel proud that she had writtenthem.

"I can hear you breathing," Terrence said as he worked on a sculpture.

Ebony was standing in the doorway of his studio while he molded a man and a panther. The panther stood on its hind legs, and the man held a spear.

"I like to watch you work. It's amazing," she remarked

as she entered the room and sat on the stool near his platform.

"Actually, it's not. The hands have a memory of their own. On abasic level, it's quite simple," he replied.

She watched him place his hands on the toy panther by his side. Even though the model was on all four legs, he was able to use it as a model for his sculpture.

"I could never do that.""Have you tried?" "No."

"Then how can you be sure?"

Before she could respond, he wiped his hand on a towel, then held it out for her to take. He led Ebony over to his prep table where he kept bricks of unrolled clay. He took down one block andbegan to wet it to loosen it up.

"Do you see my bandana?" Terrence asked."Yes. It's on the table."

"Hand it to me."

She did. He took it and stepped behind her and tied it aroundher eyes.

"What are you doing?" Ebony asked with a curious giggle."Welcome to my world," he whispered in her ear.

From behind, he placed the wet block of clay in front of her and began kneading it out of its square form into a gooey glob, then he placed her hands on it.

"Now, squeeze," Terrence told her with a light chuckle.

"Huh?" she breathed, because she hadn't heard a word he said. All she could think about was how good his body felt against hers.

Since they'd met, Terrence had been respectful. She'd gotten soused to his presence she would walk around him naked. Until one day when she had just gotten out of the shower and waltzed into the kitchen where he was eating.

"You're naked," he remarked, a mischievous grin on his face as he chewed.

She almost covered herself. "How can you tell?"

He shrugged. "Your walk. It's more sensual. It's slower when you're naked. I can tell you're comfortable with your body."

Ever since then, she would be naked almost all the time. She would fantasize about him, but she felt like it could never happen ... .

Until that moment.

The way he pressed up against her, she knew he had been having those same thoughts. But she tried to put them out of her mind and concentrate on the task at hand.

"Squeeze the clay. Get used to the feeling. Forget that you can't see it. Just feel it," he instructed, still up close to her ear.

She could feel it all right, but it wasn't clay.

Ebony did as he said. "It feels . . . gooey." She giggled.

"Maybe that's how God felt when he made us from his mind. You're doing a good job. Now round it off. Roll it on the table. Like this." He put his arms on top of hers and helped her roll the clay into a ball. "See?"

"I can feel it now," she replied.

"Good. Now I want you to make a person's face—the eyes, nose, mouth, ears. Do a complete face."

"How?" she whined.

"Just imagine a face in your mind, and your hands will mold what the mind sees. The mind is the real eye anyway, the eye itself is just a vehicle," he shared some wisdom with her.

Ebony began to feel her way across the ball of clay,

177

using her palm to gauge distance and depth. She began with the eyes, making indentations in the clay with her thumbs. Then she pinched the edge of the indentations and slightly stretched it to give the eyes a slant. She then used one hand to keep track of where the eyes were, to make sure she centered the nose a little lower. She then traced her hand down and cut a half moon smile with her pinkie nail. Ebony felt the crest of the smile and used her thumb nails to give the smile dimples.

"I think I did it!" she said, then snatched the bandana off.

She was surprised at how easy it had been. It looked like a pumpkin face, but it was the first time she had ever physically seen with her mind. "Look!"

Ebony handed it to him like a proud daughter would hand it to her father. Terrence took it in his hands and smiled.

"Wow! Okay. You did better than I thought. He's even got dimples." He smirked, rubbing his thumbs over them.

He set the clay down. "That's how you do it. You're a natural," he complimented her.

"Now you're going too far." She smirked.

"You know . . . I would love to do a statute of you," Terrence proposed.

"Me?" she echoed. "I – I . . . I don't know what to say." Terrence smiled. "Say yes."

"But I—" Ebony began to protest. He put his finger to her lips, which silenced her words but quickened her pulse.

"Really, Ebony, I've been thinking about it for a while. You're beautiful, but I don't think you know it."

He reached to caress her cheek, but Ebony gently

moved his hand and turned away. "Please, Terrence. No."

His touch felt sensual and her whole body throbbed from one caress. But she was afraid for him to feel her face. She was scared he would see that she was ugly and everything would change.

Ebony wanted to hide behind his blindness, but Terrence wouldn't let her. "What's wrong, Ebony? I can hear it in your voice."

"I . . . I . . . I can't."

"Talk to me. Why?"

"Because I'm ugly!" she blurted, and hearing it out loud made her cry. "I'm ugly, Terrence. I'm not who you think I am! I'm ugly, I'm dirty, I'm-I'm trash! Please, I don't want to do this!"

Terrence took her firmly by the wrist and pulled her to him, and she buried her face in his chest. "Shhh Ebony, don't cry. You're not ugly."

"I am!"

"No, you're not. I already know what you look like. I can tell by the way you form your words you have full, thick, African lips. The kind that white women pay big money and inject themselves to have. Collagen. You know what that is? It comes from pigs," he said with disgust. "I know you have short, kinky hair, and I know that you're more comfortable naked. You deserve to be immortalized, Ebony, because you are a beautiful black woman," he concluded in a gentle tone.

He used his thumbs to remove her tears while he worked his hands over the soft contours and curves of her high cheek-bones, her button cute nose and her wet, trembling lips. She had to fight the urge to suck his thumb.

The tremble in his touch let her know he was fighting urges, too. "Take off your clothes," Terrence demanded in a hoarse whisper.

"Terrence—"

"No words," he cut her off, with an urgency that only lust could produce.

She looked into his light eyes, and the intensity in his face madeit seem as if he were looking straight at her.

Ebony let her sweatpants and panties fall to the floor. She pulled her tank top over her head. She paused long enough to look at him before taking his hands and placing them on her breasts. Her nipples hardened as he caressed them with his thumbs, then palmed and ran his hands over them so lovingly and skillfully, she almost came on the spot.

"So beautiful," he whispered to himself as he slid his hands along the under sides of her breasts, over her cleavage, then back up to her shoulders, feeling his way along her arms until he interlaced his fingers with hers.

"Terrence, you feel so good," she gasped. "I've never been touched like this before."

His hands roamed her body, not missing a spot from head to toe. Every touch sent shivers through her until he ran his hands along her inner thighs. Ebony's entire body shuddered and she came hard. She felt light-headed.

Terrence felt her wobble and steadied her. He scooped her in hisarms and carried her across the room to his bed.

"Terrence—we can't. I—"

"Shhhh," he replied, silencing her with a gentle kiss as he laid her down.

Then he began to cover her whole body with kisses.

Ebony squirmed wildly—she had never wanted a man inside her this bad, and knowing she couldn't have him was driving her insane.

"I've wanted to do this for so long," Terrence whispered between kisses, and started sucking on her toes.

Ebony couldn't take it anymore. She arched her back and cocked her legs open, massaging her clit. "Oh, my pussy is on fire. I'm on fire," she gasped, plunging three fingers inside and taking her own breath away.

Terrence stopped and stood up, then began to undress. Ebony looked at him. "Terrence, you know we can't do this," she reminded him, damn near in tears because she wanted him that bad.

"We can if we use protection," he replied, going to his nightstand drawer, retrieving a magnum.

"But that's not one hundred percent."

"Nothing ever is. But you don't get this close to heaven without having faith," he answered. He took off his jeans and boxers. His dick stood out long, black, and thick. Pre-cum oozed from the tip of his dick in a long drip. Ebony used her finger to remove it, then sucked her finger.

"My God, I want you so bad," she gasped breathlessly.

Terrence covered his hard, black love muscle, then got down on his knees between her legs. Ebony spread her thighs from east to west, straddling the bed as if it was a continent. She couldn't wait to feel him inside of her. She grabbed his dick and guided him into her love.

"Oh Terrence!" she moaned, arching her back to meet his thrust.

"Heaven," he repeated, wrapping his arms around her and grinding her as deeply as he could.

Ebony wrapped her legs around him, urging him deeper,wanting to feel him in her stomach.

"Oh my God, it's so good!" she cooed.

"You're so good. I love you," Terrence grunted. Hearing the three words made her whole body shiver. "Tell me again," she urged.

"I love you, Ebony. I love you."

Every time he said it she came. So she came over and over. No man had ever made love to her, or made her feel loved. He sexed her until she fell asleep, her face wet with tears, and the bed wet with her juices.

When she woke up, it was well after dark. Her eyes had to adjust. When they did, she saw him at his platform hard at work. His back was to her, so she lay there admiring his body. She had never seen him naked. His body was slim and sinewy, but muscular. He had the body of a marathon runner.

"Good evening, sleepy head," he greeted her without turning around.

"You know me so well, it's scary." She sighed like a woman secured.

"It's not that. It's your breathing pattern. I can hear when it changes," he explained, then added, "Come over here. I have something to show you."

Ebony got out of bed, still feeling the throb of his rhythm in her pussy, making her walk sensually. She wrapped her arms around his waist as she peered around him. What she saw made her heart skip a beat.

It was her.

"It's beautiful," she remarked, admiringly. He tipped her face to his.

"You're beautiful. You can't have one without the other."

She looked at the clay reflection of herself. She was nude, her body shapely and flawless, with her arms in the air as if she were declaring her freedom. Her head was thrown back, a look of ecstasy on her face.

"I love it, Terrence. Thank you. I don't know what to say." "You've already said it," he replied. Kissing her passionately,

he added, "I bet you don't know where I got that face from."

She peered at herself closely. It was her fuck face. She laughed and hit him playfully.

"You sure you're blind?" she joked.

"To everything but you," he replied smoothly.

They shared a tender moment of silence until Terrence broke the embrace. "I–umm–want to talk to you about something," he began, putting a little distance between them.

Ebony sensed something was wrong. "Okay," she replied, her tone colored with subtle anxiety.

"I . . . I've got an opportunity to move to Italy."

As soon as he said it, her heart deflated. "I . . . understand." "You do?" he replied, as if relieved at not having to explain. "Yes," Ebony answered, fighting back tears. "You're going to leave me and go to Italy."

"What? No! I want you to move to Italy with me," heexclaimed.

It took a minute for his words to penetrate her assumed sadness."You what!"

He stepped back over to her and took her in his arms.

"I wantyou to move to Italy with me. I want you to be my wife."

The last word made her breathless. "Nooooo Terrence . . ."

"No?" he repeated, feeling almost crushed.

"No, no, no. I mean, yes! I meant no, I can't believe it!" shestammered, so happy, that nothing coming out of her mouth made sense until she shouted, "Yes, Terrence! I'll be your wife!" She jumped into his arms and wrapped her legs around his waist, but it caught him off guard, and he stumbled then tumbled to the floor laughing.

"See, you got me weak in the knees." He laughed.

Ebony leaned down and kissed him. "Your knees ain't what I need right now. You better have a whole box of those gold wrappers!"

The next few weeks were all about planning and packing. Ebony couldn't stop thanking God. Her every breath became a prayer.

"Thank you, God. You saved me, Lord. You saved me," she would whisper whenever the spirit hit her.

"Baby, I've got to go to Milan and take care of some last minute details," Terrence told her one morning when she woke up.

"Okay, baby."

Terrence smiled, like it was bubbling out of him.

"No baby, better than okay. I'm not making any promises, but there are doctors over there, doctors that are making major breakthroughs concerning AIDS and HIV."

Before he could finish, she hugged his neck. Even hearing the words were too good to be true. A cure? Ebony had never even dared to let herself think of one. But to hear the words made her heart overflow. "I love you, Terrence!"

"Just don't get your hopes up. No promises."

"The only promise I need is that you'll never leave me!"
"I promise."

And then it was over.

The end came on the prettiest day. The sun was shining and the birds were singing and Terrence's, "I love you, Ebony," was still echoing in her ears after they rode to the airport in a taxi, and she was on her way back to the apartment.

"Is it the waaayy, you loooove—me, baby," she sang softly to herself along with Jill Scott in her head.

Everything was perfect. Too perfect, but she had never known perfection to realize it. She allowed herself to dream of having a child for the first time since she was little and would carry dolls under her shirt, and act as if she were giving birth. When her life became ugly, there was no room for children . . . or dreams for thatmatter.

But Terrence's love had changed all that and given her a reason to love life for the first time.

She went back to the apartment to finish packing. Ebony had already packed up the stereo. She turned on the TV for comfort.

"We interrupt this program for a breaking news bulletin," the reporter announced.

Ebony was only half paying attention. She was too busy preparing for her new life.

"A Boeing 747 that departed from Newark's Liberty National Airport en route to Italy has reportedly crashed into the Atlantic Ocean . . ."

When she heard the word "Italy", she looked up and her mind replayed the entire sentence. She turned toward the

TV, feeling a sick tightening in her stomach.

"Flight 817 destined for Italy apparently was experiencing engine trouble. Details are sketchy, but we do know that the coast guard has determined that there is no way anyone could have survived the initial impact and explosion . . ."

At first she felt nothing. Numb. Like she had lost any connection to reality, and all she could hear was, "No one could survive, no one could survive . . . no one could—"

"No," she whispered, shaking her head, refusing to believe.

No one could survive.

"Nooooooo!" she screamed, covering her ears as if she could block the sound of her own thoughts.

She grabbed the nearest object, hoisted it over her head, and smashed the flat screen into a thousand short circuiting pieces. "Noooooo!" she continued to scream.

The moment her shock, anger, and pain settled down, she realized what she'd used to bust up the TV.

Her statue.

It lay in the ruined TV, no longer looking like her hands were raised in victory. They looked like she had thrown up both her arms in resigned defeat. The ecstatic look on her face now looked dazed and pained. If she had been floating, she now came crashing back to earth, hard.

Her tears were uncontrollable, unstoppable, and drove her into a fetal position.

How?

That was the one word that haunted her mind. How, not why, because she felt like she already knew why. The why in Ebony's mind was simple. She was cursed. God had singled her out from birth to step on, kick, berate, and punish. To dangle happiness in her face, and then snatch it away was worse than never knowing happiness at all.

How?

The sun set and rose with Ebony still in a fetal position. She hadn't slept a wink, nor moved a muscle. She felt as dead as any corpse could be. Slowly, she peeled herself from the floor. The pain she was feeling, she wanted someone else to feel. If God could send her man to a watery death, she was determined to send another man to a wetter one.

She showered, but instead of washing away the dirt, she washedaway anything clean, pure.

"This is the bitch you made, so this is the bitch you get," Ebony spat coldly, directing her blasphemous prayer to the heavens.

She grabbed a short dress, so short her bare ass cheeks were almost exposed for the world to kiss. Her heels screamed, "fuck me" and the fire-red lipstick she put on made her mouth resemble abull's-eye for a big black dick. Ebony stopped in front of the mirror and saw herself. In her own eyes, she saw what she intendedto do.

"NO!" she said to her reflection.

The image gazing back at her was the only goodness left, and Ebony was the evil twin.

"We have to stop this . . . now," she told herself.

Ebony pulled out her phone and called the suicide hotline.

"This is the suicide helpline. My name is Cathy, what's yours?" the sweet, comforting voice said.

"Ebony."

"That's a pretty name, Ebony. I really am glad you called.

Would you like to talk?"

Ebony squeezed her eyes so tight that a tear escaped. She thentook a deep breath. "I need help."

****

CHAPTER TWENTY-THREE

BLESS . . . BEFORE EBONY

He watched the pretty woman who reminded him of Alicia Keys like a hawk would a mouse scampering across the meadow. The hustle and bustle of New York Penn

Station never distracted him as he eyed her from across the room.

Everything she did was a dead giveaway. First, she had no luggage other than the leather satchel she kept in her grip. Her nervousness expressed itself in the jiggle of her bouncing leg, a dancer's leg, thick and brown. Her neck constantly rolled from left to right, and whenever a cop came through, she looked ready to take off running.

His eyes went to the satchel, salivating with greed. His mind fully preoccupied with its contents. The anticipation was killing him, but he was determined to find out.

"Now boarding for Newark, Trenton, and

Philadelphiaaaa," the raspy-voiced woman announced over the loud speaker.

When he saw her get up, he did too. She was so phat in her white skirt and wedge-heeled sandals that every man she passed grunted, grinned, or strained his neck for one more peek at the Buffy-sized ass. He rushed to the counter and placed his money in the slot.

"One way to Philly," he requested, choosing Philadelphia because his gut told him she wasn't going farther than that.

The nasal-voiced white woman replied, "That bus is leaving now."

"Yeah, and I can too if you'd hurry the hell up!" he spat back, his tone a lot less harsh than the words themselves conveyed.

The woman took one look at this stone-faced black man, and decided sarcasm would not be a good idea. She took the moneyand generated his ticket.

"Have a nice trip," she said, but the tone sounded like, "Go to hell!"

He took the ticket. "You, too," he responded, and her flippant expression said she definitely got it. As the loudspeaker announced, "Last call for Newark Penn Station, Trenton, and Philadelphia," he jogged off.

Just as the barrel chested African American driver was thunkingaway the last of his cigarette, he reached the bus. The driver took one look at his physique, his black, no-named boots and khaki pants, smirked and remarked, "Just coming home, huh? Welcome back to the so called free world." He chuckled and took his ticket. He had picked up countless newly released prisoners with the very same outfit on.

"No doubt. 'Preciate that."

He stepped onto the half-packed bus. There were plenty of seats, but he was only interested in one. The seat beside her. He spotted her midway to the back and scanned the bus to see if anyone was riding shotgun with her in the shadows. No one fit the description.

"Is that seat taken?" he smiled.

When she looked up into that sexy smile that reminded her of Boris Kodjoe, along with the body that made him look like an action figure, she couldn't say anything but, "No. No, it's not."

He sat down as the bus pulled off. "I'm Bless," he introduced himself, extending his hand.

"Yes you are," she flirted, looking him over like an all-you-can-eat menu.

He chuckled. "Only because this seat wasn't taken."

She blushed. "I like that. That was smooth. I'm Dominique."

He eyed her carefully. "That's a beautiful name. It fits you," Bless remarked.

As the bus roared up the highway, their conversation went from general to specific.

"So, how long have you been dancing?"

"Wow. Is it that obvious?" Dominique couldn't help but giggle.

Bless shrugged. "It's your walk, your body, and those pretty toes. No disrespect, but, I'd definitely pay to see you in a thong." He smirked.

Her smile said, *The money on those booty shots was well spent*. But she replied, "I just recently started dancing.

I like it, but it's only to help me over the hump, you know? I dance at a club in Manhattan. It's called The Cherry."

Bless nodded and said, "Who am I to judge?"

Dominique continued. "So what about you? How long did you do?"

Bless laughed. "I did two this time, six the last." "Who am I to judge?" She winked.

"Is it that obvious?" He joked.

"Yeah. You have that fresh out of prison glow. You know the one I'm talking aobut," she commented. "And plus, are you forgetting that you are wearing prison gear?"

"Oh, so you got jokes," he challenged.

"Duuhhh! Like I said, have you forgotten that you are wearing prison gear?"

"Oh, and she's woman enough to repeat herself." Bless grinned.

She licked her lips seductively. "Oh trust, I'm definitely woman enough. I would ask you if you are man enough, but, I don't even know you like that." She wasn't going to let him know that she was turned on by his physique and of course the fresh out of prison glow. And the thought that his dick hadn't been up in no pussy for years had her wanting to roll the dice. As far as she was concerned, this was her lucky day.

"Shit, this bus is like Vegas. What happens on the bus stays on the bus," Bless whispered in her ear while he traced a finger up her thigh.

"Don't do that. Keep your hands to yourself," she protested softly. But it was obvious to them both that she didn't mean it.

"Ma, don't front. You know you want me as bad as I

want you. I just wanna fuck that pussy from the back that's all. You know I'm fresh out and gotta huge nut to release," he whispered, sliding his hand between her thighs and rubbing her camel toe through her panties. He knew he was in there when he felt the wetness leaking through. "I know you want to enjoy cumming all over my face, and then take all this dick like the bad bitch you are."

By the time he finished talking, he had two fingers in her pussy and his thumb massaging her clit. Dominique had cocked one leg over his and was biting her bottom lip to keep from crying out.

"I dare you to show me what you're working with," she challenged him, but kept her tone low and sensual.

Bless didn't hesitate to unbutton his fly and pull out his rock hard nine-inches. Even in the dark, she could see how fat and thick it was. She gripped it and gave it a lustful squeeze.

"Damn, you got me wet as fuck. I'm damn near leaking," Dominique remarked, voice quivering. "What do you plan on doing about it?"

"Come on, let's go to the bathroom," Bless suggested.

Dominique got up and headed for the bathroom on wobbly legs, and it wasn't because of the motion of the bus. As turned on as she was, she still kept the satchel tight under her arm.

Bless waited a few minutes, then went behind her. Most of the other few passengers were asleep, except a middle-aged Spanish woman who gave Bless a look like she wanted to be next.

When he pulled open the door, Dominique was braced against the sink, her skirt up around her waist and her panties pulled to the side, fingering herself.

"What took you so long?" she quivered, on the edge of cumming.

Bless squatted down in front of her. He had a tongue like a lizard, so as soon as his tongue met her clit, she leapt to the tip of her toes and blasted off like a rocket.

"I'm coming alreadyyyyyyyy," she squealed, her body jerkingto the rhythm of an explosion.

Bless tongue-fucked her deep, and sucked her pussy until she came all over his nose, lips, and chin.

"No more, please, no more," she panted, looking down at him like a woman possessed. "Put that big-ass dick in me, baby. Fuck me."

Bless wanted to fuck her so bad, he thought he might bust off just thinking about it. He hadn't had pussy in two years, and Dominique's shaven pussy looked fat and juicy and he almost gavein. But he had a plan.

He stood up. "Hol' up, ma. You hear that?" "Hear what?"

"Yo, we betta get back to our seat. We don't want to draw a lot of attention."

Dominique wanted to protest, but when he mentioned attention, her paranoia kicked in, just like Bless hoped it would.

She sucked her teeth. "Maybe you're right."

They went back to their seats. Dominique draped her legs over Bless's lap, rubbing her thigh against his hardened print.

"Boy, that was a wild as fuck! You know you a fool for that performance! I never did anything like this before," Dominique cooed.

Bless chuckled. "I wish I had your ass stretched out on a bed, because you got that snapper." He winked, making her blush, then added, "Can I tell you something?"

She looked at him curiously. "What?"

Bless looked into her eyes and said, "He doesn't care nothin' about you."

"Who?"

He smiled. "Come on, ma. I know the game, and I peeped game as soon as I saw you. I put many bitches on the bus with a package before. It's obvious that you carrying. Nothing about you says you belong on a Greyhound. So if it's obvious to me, who else you think it's obvious to?" Bless asked, breaking it down to her.

Her heart beat faster as she looked around the bus with new eyes.

"Ma, any of these muhfuckas could be a cop just waitin' to see where you get off, and pop your ass for trafficking. Feel me? Because as long as you on this bus, technically, you haven't trafficked. But once you step off, then it's over!"

He was lying through his teeth, but to her virgin ears it was the gospel truth. Tears welled up in her eyes. Bless cupped her chin and turned her face to him.

"What's wrong, ma?"

"He—he said he loved me," she sobbed.

Bless had to fight back his laughter. "Does putting you in a situation that could cost you twenty years feel like love?"

"Twenty years!" she shrieked.

"Shhh, ma, calm down. Listen," he said, looking around. "This is what we gonna do. I'm from Philly. You get off with me. We go and get a room while I wait on my peoples to rent a car. Then I'll drive you back to New York. How does that sound?"

Dominique's gut was telling her no, but she kept hearing the echo in her ears, "Twenty years! Twenty years! Twenty years!"

Seeing her teetering on the edge of yes, he put the icing on the cake. He slid his hands up her skirt and caressed her still wet pussy.

"I got you, ma. Besides, I want to put this anaconda up in you the way I wanted to in that little-ass bathroom," Bless gamed. He felt her pussy muscles twitch with anticipation.

"Are you sure?"

Bless smiled a smile that he knew could make a bitch cum. "No doubt."

******

As soon as they hit the room, Bless was all over Dominique. "Baby, wait, let me . . . take a shower," she managed to protest between kisses.

"Fuck that, I like it raw. Bend over," he demanded, bending her over the bed.

"Ummmmm, talk like that makes my pussy wet," she cooed.

Bless slid her panties aside and dropped his pants down around his ankles. He plowed into her tight, wet pussy with every hard inch, making her scream out in pleasure and pain.

"Fuck! Yeah, nigga, do this pussy right! Fuck it good,

fuck it gooood!" she urged, throwing her pussy back like a porn star.

He cocked one of her legs up on the bed; the angle made him bang her walls out.

"Da–da–da–daddy waiiiiiit!"

"Naw bitch, you wanted it. Now take this dick!"

The loud smacking gave Bless a rush. Every stroke seemed to make her cum, wetting/drenching/flooding his dick to the point where her cream dripped down his balls.

"I feel it in my stomach!" Dominique cried out.

Bless laid her on the bed, head dangling off the edge, legs thrown over his shoulders as he banged her until she thought she would pass out.

"Pl–pl–please cum, baby," she begged.

Instead, Bless stopped. Panting, he looked down at her face. "You're beautiful, you know that?"

Dominique blushed as she tried to catch her breath. "Thank you

. . . you know, I'm glad I met you.""Don't be."

Dominique frowned slightly. "Why would you—"

He put a finger to her lips. "Because this is an ugly game, baby, and I'm a monster. But don't worry—it was over for you anyway. If I wouldn't have got you someone else would have," he said softly, then he gripped her neck and began to squeeze.

At first she liked it, until it got to the point where she couldn't breathe. Her eyes bucked, and she tried to claw at his hands, face, anything, to get him off her. But with her head hanging off the bed, it was hard to do so. She kicked her legs. Her brown eyes frantic with a pleading look that asked, *Why?*

Bless choked her until her eyes lost its light and her limbs wentlimp. He got up, his hard dick pulling out of her still sloppy, wet pussy. As soon as he pulled up his pants he grabbed the satchel anddumped the contents on the bed. A wad of money and a football- sized bag duct taped all around tumbled out. He cut open thepackage expecting to find coke or heroin, but all he found were pills. Lots and lots of round, white pills, slightly bigger than aspirin.

"What the fuck is this!" he spat, looking at her as if she could answer. "I can't believe this! Dumb bitch! You was mulin' Excedrin?" he yelled out. Bless fumed as he started to throw the pills at her in frustration, but something told him 'don't do it.' He got dressed and put the money and pills back in the satchel. In the morning they would find her body, but by then he'd be out of Philly and back home in Newark.

Besides, he was living on borrowed time, so he really didn'tgive a fuck.

CHAPTER TWENTY-FOUR

EBONY . . . THE BEGINNING

I'm glad you decided to come, Ebony." "I hope that I'll feel the same way."

Ebony looked around the office thinking, *So this is what a psychiatrist's office looks like.* In her mind she pictured something more formal. The place looked like a study. Mahogany paneling, book cases on two walls, and of course, the famous couch, which she was sitting on.

The psych, looking like an older Denzel Washington, sat in a comfortable looking arm chair, legs crossed, notepad balanced on his knee. Whenever the conversation lulled, the only sound was the ticking of the grandfather clock in the corner, which was soothing to Ebony.

"Is this your first time seeing a psychiatrist?"

Ebony nodded, her head lowered as if ashamed of eye contact. "It's okay, Ebony. I'm here to help you," the doctor assured her,

his tone as warm as a cup of tea. "Let's begin with the most important matter. Why do you want to kill yourself?"

There was a short uncomfortable silence. "Because I have nothing to live for," she replied. "I see . . . and your family, how would they feel?" "I–I don't have a family," she answered.

"I'm sorry to hear that. I too, lost my family in a car accident,"he informed her, attempting to bond.

For some reason, the attempt irked Ebony. Just because he had pain of his own, didn't mean he was an expert on hers.

She looked up for the first time. "My family was taken fromme," she replied.

"How old were you?" "Four . . . four years old."

Would you like to tell me about it?" the psych probed. Ebony shook her head.

"Ebony, I can't help you if you don't talk to me. I think this was very traumatic for you, and may hold the keys to many things. So please . . . talk to me," he urged.

Ebony twiddled with her thumbs for several moments. Finally, she took a deep breath and went back to the time that started it all .. .

"You're not taking my babies away from me!" the bone skinny woman screamed out in anguish.

Boc! Boc! Boc!

And then she let the pistol speak for her, making people in the Department of Family Services scatter, screaming and ducking. On her hip was a one year old and hiding in the corner was a four- year-old Ebony.

The white woman, her social worker, cowered behind her desk."Please Mrs. James, this is not necessary!"

"Shut up, bitch, before I put a goddamn cap in your ass!" Mrs.

James barked.

"Hey! Put down that gun!" a black man who favored George Jefferson demanded.

Boc! Boc!

"Aaaarrrrgggh!" he bellowed, all thoughts of being a hero disappearing once the two bullets hit him in the shoulder and chest. Mrs. James walked over and stood over him, aiming the gun in his face. "You people think you can just take my family from me?

What gives you the right to decide? You ain't God, goddammit!"

The social worker's face turned beet red, and warm liquid trickled down her leg. She was afraid that if she said something,

Mrs. James would kill them all. But that still didn't stop her from trying to reason with her.

"Mrs. James, what else can we do? You have AIDS! You are full blown, and only time will tell how much longer—"

"Shut up!" Miss James screamed, not wanting to hear the truth, so she didn't have to face it.

The truth was, she wasn't mad at the social worker, she was mad at herself. Mad that she had allowed sweet words and a moment of lust to become a virtual death sentence. Mad that she brought two kids into the world to suffer along with her. A part of her wanted to kill the kids too, so they would never know the pain and agony.

"Mama, look!" young Ebony pointed at the window.

Mrs. James looked towards the windows and saw police cruisers surrounding the building. The shooting had been reported and help had quickly responded. A tear formed in her eye.

"Mama, don't cry. I love you," Ebony said, hugging her thigh. "I love you too, baby," Mrs. James replied.

She knew it would be double hard for Ebony, because she knew Ebony wouldn't grow up to be pretty, and an unattractive woman in America was doomed, not to mention one that was HIV positive as well.

"Please, Mrs. James, think of your kids," the social worker pleaded.

"Shut up!" Mrs. James barked.

Boc!

She let off a shot on impulse, not meaning to, but her fingers were on the trigger. The bullet pierced the social worker's dome, leaving a gaping hole in her forehead and a surprised look on her face as her brains exploded from the back of her head and splattered blood across the room, some landing on Ebony's face.

The warm plasma took her by surprise, and the image of the dying woman would stay forever in her memory. Mrs. James didn't have time to react to her fatal mistake as the police came bursting through the door.

"At–at that point, my mother knew it was over. She knew the police wouldn't spare her . . . she handed my baby brother to me and said, "Take care of him," before she turned to run out of the office," Ebony told the doctor. "I can still hear that officer's voice." Ebony cringed.

"I dare you to move!"

"Drop. That. Gun," the officer warned, but Mrs. James was past the point of caring. She was about to go to jail and rot and die a horrible death. She'd much rather get it over right then and there.

"Fuck you!" she screamed before she opened fire. Boc! Boc! Click!

She only got off two shots before her clip was empty. But it didn't matter. The police lit her up like a Christmas tree, hittingher countless times. The bloody mist from her body spewing blood looked like smoke rising.

"Maaaaaaaaaaaa!" Ebony yelled.

Mrs. James flopped back, flipping over a desk and landing on her side. The only thing that saved young Ebony was the smile on her mother's face.

That smile made her love death.

The police took the young baby from her.

"Jermaine, no! Gimme back my brother! Gimme back my Jermaine!" she cried out. Her cries fell on deaf ears.

When the police took the kids out of the building, they put them in separate cars. Ebony squirmed out of her seat belt, threw open the door, and ran.

"Hey!" the male social worker yelled.

The car her little brother sat in was leaving the parking lot and turning onto the street but there was another car that headed back towards her. Ebony knew one thing. If she couldn't have her brother, she'd rather have her mama's smile.

She jumped in front of the car. Skkkkrrrrrreeeech!

"After that, it was just . . . pain. But it was better than feelingalone, you know?" Ebony described her feelings.

The psych nodded and wrote on his pad. "And at that momentof impact, was death what you wanted?"

"Yes."

"I see. And what happened after that?"

"I woke up in the hospital," Ebony replied, hating to

203

relive the moment she first met Miss Cat.

"Ebony? Ebony, sweetheart, can you hear me? Why won't you talk to me?" the nurse questioned, wearing a pleasant smile.

Ebony had just awakened from the accident. Everything ached, but nothing more than her heart. She realized she was all alone in the world, and her sadness wouldn't let her speak. She gazed up at the nurse, and the heavy-set light-skinned woman beside her. The white woman gave off a good feel, but the black woman, the one who looked like Della Reese, gave off such a compelling negative vibe it was like a stench, despite her jovial look and kind smile.

"The poor child is traumatized," the black woman theorized, then looked at Ebony and added, "But don't you worry. The Lord'll make it all better." She took Ebony's hand, but Ebony pulled it away and turned her head.

"Oh, Ebony, don't be like that. This is Miss Catherine, and she's going to be your new foster mother," the nurse announced.

Ebony's answer was tears that trickled from her eyes and dripped onto her pillow.

"Her name was Miss Cat, and she was the worst thing that ever happened to me," Ebony explained, now strong enough to speak freely about her past life with Satan's sister.

"Did she . . . abuse you?" the psych questioned carefully.

Ebony nodded. "In more ways than one. She sold young girls to neighborhood pedophiles. Her house was like a brothel. Sometimes I think the state knew, because they only sent certain kinds of girls there."

"That couldn't be true. You're saying the state knowingly allowed kids to be sexually abused?" he prodded.

"You'd be surprised. But it also did something else."

"What?"

Ebony looked him in the eyes, a trace of a smirk on her lips. "It made me commit my first murder."

CHAPTER SEVEN

BACK TO BLESS ... THE MOMENT THAT STARTED IT ALL

Bless was back in prison . . .*Bare chested and clad only in his boxers, he was in his cell with his back against the wall. His whole body was tense* with anger as he looked out into what seemed to be a sea of police gathered outside his cell.

"Come on, you bitch ass muhfuckas. Bring it!" Bless roared,*his voice bouncing off the walls like bass.*

"It doesn't have to go down like this," the head CO proposed. "You know what you need to do."

"Fuck that! I'm tired of this shit! I'm tired!" "Go! Go! Go!" the head CO barked.

Two by two the police ran up in Bless's cell, and two by two he was laying them out. Jabs, rights, lefts, hooks, uppercuts, one after another, each blow literally exploding their heads. Bless's body was covered in sweat and blood, but still they kept coming. "You're no match for all of us!" a CO cackled, right before Bless cut him with a left that *cracked his jaw.*

Bless's arms began to tire. "You . . . will . . . never . . . beat . . . me!" he growled, exhausted.

But then they swarmed in. "Noooo!" he barked.

"Hold him! Hold him! Here comes the nurse!"

A chubby white lady came in, gloved and masked up, holding a needle in her hand. "Keep him still," she instructed.

Bless struggled, but he was too winded to fight. "Get off me!"

"Bring it down, inmate." She snatched the plastic wrap fromthe needle with her teeth.

"Bitch, fuck you too!"

She shook her head, then tapped the needle and squirted a splash to remove any lethal air bubbles. The officers held him tightly as she stuck the needle in his vein. He was extremely tense. His veins were throbbing all along his arms like cracks in a slab ofice.

"Okay, we're done," she told them. Then added, "See, it wasn'tso bad."

Bless spat dead in her face.

"Oh my God! Oh my God! He spit on me!" the nurse shrieked, running in place in a frantic panic.

"Boy, I'ma kill you!" one of the redneck officers screamed as he began beating Bless in the head with his baton.

Even though every blow made Bless feel like his head was aboutto burst, he laughed maniacally. "That's what I want! You can't make me live! You can't!"

"Be careful what you ask for," one of the officers said, sticking a gun in Bless's face.

Boom!

Bless bolted up, sweating like he was melting. Neecie, the flylittle redbone beside him sat up too.

"What's wrong?" she asked, urgency and panic filled her tone.

It took a minute for him to focus, to make sure he wasn't still in a cell. He looked around and lay back down. "Nothin'," he mumbled.

"Nothin'?" she echoed. "Baby, it's obvious you had a bad dream, but it's okay now. You're home where you belong. I missed you, boy," Neecie said soothingly as she lay her head onhis chest.

"Yeah? I guess that's why you wrote me every day and kept all that money on my books, huh?" He was smiling, but she knew he meant it.

Neecie sat up and leaned on her arms like a kickstand. "Don't start, Bless, okay? It ain't like I locked you up. I mean, come on. Really? You was gone for two years. And shit happens. I told you that I don't do the prison relationships, and as for money, I was strugglin'. In case you didn't know, two kids keep a bitch broke, and you damn sure wasn't sending me any money," she ranted at the same time, glad to get it off her chest.

Bless continued to smile as he tweaked her nipple playfully. "Naw, ma, I'm just fuckin' wit' you. I ain't mad at you. I mean, at first I was, but I got over it. You know, I matured a little bit. Bottom line is Daddy's home now," he said as he pulled her down for a kiss.

Satisfied, Neecie laid her head back on his chest and fondled hisdick. "Daddy's home is right. But Bless, tell me something. Why you all of a sudden wanna fuck raw?

When you were home before, you used to always strap up," she asked.

"Because I wasn't ready to be a daddy. Now I am."

"Uh-uh, boy, don't even go there. Two is enough." Neecielooked at him skeptically.

"Shit, you had that nigga's babies. You can have mine."

Neecie sucked her teeth. "Whateva, boy. It is what it is. You here now, so let it go."

Bless lay back, relaxing in the sexual afterglow. He had been home two days, and had yet to do anything with the pills. Truth be told, he didn't know what to do with them. But he knew he had to make a move because he was down to his last hundred dollars.

"Ma, let me ask you somethin'. What you know about pills?" Bless questioned.

"What kind of pills?"

He didn't want to admit he didn't know what he had, so he fudged. "The white kind you get high on."

Neecie snickered. "Wow that really narrows it down." He had to laugh, too.

"Anyway, I don't know 'bout that shit, but JT do. He canhandle that for you." She told him.

Bless flexed his jaw with subtle annoyance. It wasn't just because JT was his man and they did time together, they hustled together and he had gotten his girl pregnant—twice. Now he had to ask the nigga for help? His pride wasn't feeling Neecie's idea.

Neecie felt his vibe. "Look, Bless. JT and me don't even deal like that no more. He don't even take care of his sons. But when it come to that street shit, JT be on his game. I know you're thinking that I disrespected you by—"

"I don't want to talk about that shit right now."

"Why not? We gonna have to talk about it eventually."

"Yo, I need to move these pills. Get the nigga over here."

THE END

Neecie signed the Valentine's Day Card for Bless, applied red lipstick and kissed the inside of the card. She stood back to admire her handiwork. Satisfied, she smiled.

"Okay." She sighed. She looked in the mirror and liked what she saw. Her curls were falling just right, her make-up was flawless and she was loving her new, long lashes. She picked up her cell phone, puckered up and snapped a selfie.

Her baby started whining. "Wait a minute, baby. Mommy will be right there. Let me shoot this video for Uncle Bless. He gonna be your new daddy."

She hit the record button on the phone and held it up. "Happy Valentine's babeeeee. And I am so glad you are home. Even though you said you don't hate me, I know you do. I would hate me too. But you gotta understand how hard it is out here trying to survive. I know I did you wrong, but at the time it was the best that I could do for me.

Anyhoo, I hope this will help! It took me a while, and even though you call me a hood rat, I am not a dummy. I pulled some strings and guess what, bae? I found your sister! Yaaayyy me! Her name is Ebony James and her last known address is inside the envelope. She has been right here under our noses. I hope this will help you forgive me a little bit. No. Fuck that. A whole lot! Just know that I am always her for you, bae. Down for whateva. I hope that you find her.

Happy Valentine's! Muah! Tonight I'ma make you a special dinner. So be back by 7:00 okay? Love you! I can't wait to see what you got me! But in the meantime, in between time, all of thiswill be waiting on you."

She used the camera to scan over her naked body. She giggled, and then put it in a text message and hit the send button.

READING GROUP DISCUSSION QUESTIONS

1. Do you think it is possible to fall in love instantly the way Ebony and Bless did? Why or why not?

2. In Chapter four, Ebony and Bless both said, "Promise me, no matter wh-what happens, you'll never—" How do you think they filled in the blank?

3. Do you think Ebony was out of her mind to go on the robberies and killing sprees with Bless?

4. What were your overall feelings for these two Thuggz?

5. Would you have preferred to see them live or die? Please explain.

6. Can you justify Bless's anger toward Neecie?

7. Even though Bless and Ebony knowingly spread their virus? Were they still likeable? Please explain.

8. Do you agree that many people are having unprotected sex in this day and time? If so, what would you suggest be done to curtail this dangerous act?

9. If you could rewrite any of the scenes, which scene would it be? Explain.

10. Which character resonated with you the most? Why?

NEW STREET LIT TITLES

FROM WAHIDA CLARK PRESENTS INNOVATIVE PUBLISHING